## Behind the Closed Door . . .

Heavy footsteps outside on the linoleum, and Simon's breath coming in curses. Grey shook once and froze. His hands had just found the handle of a knife. He suddenly found himself enraged, enveloped by the killing madness of an animal at the point of death. In his mind was an image of his family, Judith and Katy, alone in this house, with Grey dead and Simon still alive. That was the one thing he couldn't let happen. His hand tightened on the handle of the knife. When the door opened he would be on Simon so fast the two of them would die together. Grey was all fury now, no more logic. . . . He waited for the pantry door to open. . . .

**Books by Jay Brandon**

Deadbolt*
Fade the Heat*
Tripwire
Predator's Waltz*
Rules of Attraction

*Published by POCKET BOOKS

# DEAD BOLT

JAY BRANDON

POCKET BOOKS
New York London Toronto Sydney Tokyo Singapore

POCKET BOOKS, a division of Simon & Schuster Inc.
1230 Avenue of the Americas, New York, NY 10020


Published by arrangement with the author


For information address: Pocket Books, 1230 Avenue of the Americas, New York, NY 10020

ISBN: 0-671-70887-2

First Pocket Books printing July 1992

10 9 8 7 6 5 4 3 2 1



Cover illustration and design by James Lebbad

Printed in the U.S.A.

*To my parents,*
**Bob and Dorene Brandon**

# DEAD BOLT

# 1

HIS CHILD WAS ON THE LEDGE. HE COULDN'T help her. She was at the mercy of gravity and her own unreliable balance. She swayed there, delicately poised between falling one way or another, between releasing a cry or holding it. The three-foot wall, slightly taller than Katy herself, enclosed the second-story terrace. Katy had never been atop it before. All she had ever seen from the terrace was open sky. She didn't grasp the function of the wall, didn't realize that the world dropped off on the other side to the ground below. In all her short life she had never taken a long fall. There had always been someone holding her.

Grey was trapped by the woman who'd come to his front door ten minutes earlier. He was up on the terrace, lost in thought, papers spread over his lap and the chair and the small table, when he heard someone calling from below. He had gone to look over the edge, still murmuring phrases to himself. Katy came hurrying after him and he took her hand.

"Hellooo," the woman was calling from below. "Is there anyone home?"

He couldn't see her; she was on the front porch directly below his feet. "Yes?" he said helpfully. He had to say it again before she heard him and stepped out into view. When she looked up at him she shaded her face with her hand, so he still didn't get a very good look at her.

"Oh, there you are. Mr. Stanton? Are you Mr. Stanton?"

"Yes."

"Oh hello. My name is Marcie Willis—don't try to place me, we've never met before—but I know a little bit about you. Could we talk for just a minute? I hate to bother you, but it's really important, I could come back later if you'd rather, but let me warn you I will be back. I'm sorry but I'm going to have to pester you a little, I'll try to make it as painless as possible—"

Sometime during this recitation Grey had picked up Katy, as if the baby could anchor him in the whitewater rush of words. Katy leaned away from him, completely unafraid of the drop, just wanting to see this strange intruder.

"So could I? Talk to you?"

Grey would rather not have been interrupted, but she seemed persistent. "All right," he said, "just a minute, I'll—"

"Oh, that's all right, don't bother, I'll come up there. Is this door open?" She disappeared back under the eave and he heard the doorknob rattle. Marcie popped back into view. "It is. Don't worry, I'll come up there, I don't want to put you to any trouble."

"It's no—" Grey began, but she vanished again and he heard the front door slam. So now this stranger was in his house and he wasn't. He tried to remember if the living room was a mess and what valuables were in plain sight. He was torn between going to the head of the stairs to meet her and staying at the ledge to make sure she didn't come running out carrying an armload of silver or the television.

"What do you think, Katy, can we trust her?" he asked his daughter. But Katy was little more than a year old, not ready to deal with such an abstract question, so she didn't waste any of her tiny vocabulary on it. She stared back at him, her blue eyes wide.

Grey felt as he always had when waiting for a new client to be ushered into his office, slightly nervous but confident of his power to comfort. He realized he had missed that feeling. No one had sought him out in a while.

He carried Katy to the terrace doors and was grateful to hear Marcie's step on the interior stairs. "Out here," he called. A moment later she appeared at the inside door of the game room.

"Oh, good," she said. She wasn't the least bit out of breath. She hurried around the pool table toward him and Grey stepped back out into the sunshine.

"You have a great house. I just love it. Hi, cutie."

The last remark was to the baby. Katy, one hand clasping her father's collar, stared at her with the fascination of a baby who didn't see many strangers. Marcie was not much over twenty, Grey guessed, and youthfully pretty, but she wasn't distinctive except for the vitality she projected. Her cheeks were flushed from her run up the stairs and she leaned forward slightly, which gave her the impression of still advancing even after she had stopped. Her dark hair was pulled back in a ponytail. Her eyes were a lighter brown, her nose small and straight. She wore jeans, tennis shoes and a college T-shirt, and looked good in that outfit, a trick only the young and fit can pull off.

Katy reached toward her, saying something, and Marcie touched the baby's face, laughing. "Oh, you know you're a cutie, don't you?" Katy laughed and leaned further out of Grey's arms. Marcie took her, held her for only a moment while they smiled at each other, then set her down. The process of taking the baby from

Grey's arms back to the floor was almost continuous.

The silence suddenly seemed voluminous. Even Katy was unwilling to break it, though she clearly didn't like being on her feet again. Grey picked her up and motioned his guest out onto the terrace. "My wife's out shopping right now, so if you're doing some kind of survey—"

"No, no, it's just you I want to talk to—"

Marcie blinked when she stepped outside. It was only March, but March in central Texas is a bright month, the sun all the stronger for being unexpected. Grey and Marcie sat on lawn chairs in the center of the small terrace. Grey continued to hold Katy until the baby became restless. He set her down then, careful to see that the tar paper shingles that floored the terrace weren't too hot or rough for her feet. Katy wandered away, and Grey listened to Marcie.

She told him her name again and added, "I'm a student at U.T." The University of Texas was only fifteen miles away in Austin, so she hadn't come far. "I'm a senior this year, sociology major—" She grimaced, as many students will when forced to admit their major field of study. "—and I'm doing a sort of thesis, in which you'll be instrumental, and I just wondered if I could talk to you for a minute?" When he didn't respond immediately she added, "To tell the truth, I'm also thinking about going to law school myself when I graduate, so I hoped I could kill two birds with one stone and learn more about how the law works for my own purposes."

"I see," Grey said unenthusiastically.

A beautiful day rested lightly on the earth around them. Trees were cautiously displaying their second buds of the year. A warm week in January had fooled them, as it always did, into putting forth a first set of buds that had been killed by the last freezing temperatures of the season. The temperature today was in the seventies, and the trees were regaining their confidence. Their boldness had prompted other stirrings in the earth. The view from the terrace to the nearby hills was turning green.

Katy stretched her arms and squinted at the sun. It was only the second spring of her life, but she had more confidence in it than did the trees. Trying to capture the warmth of the sun, she began hopping, lost her balance, and sat down hard. When she knew she wasn't hurt she said "Boom" and laughed. Grey turned to look at her and laughed too before turning back to Marcie. Katy picked herself up and walked farther away.

"What I want to do in this paper is look at the criminal justice system from behind the scenes," Marcie said. She hung her purse on the back of her chair and took a small notebook from it. "I'm sure you've read that generally speaking cops and crooks come from the same level of society. Now, that's not true of criminals and their lawyers, but I wonder if sometimes a rapport can develop between a lawyer and a particular client." She smiled. "My professor suggested my theme should be that lawyers are just crooks who had the money to go to law school." Her smile didn't quite disarm the remark. Grey smiled back. "Could you tell me a little about your own background?" she concluded.

Marcie stared at him intently, pen held above her notebook. It was flattering to see such a voluble person sitting mute, waiting for him to speak. "What would you like to know?" he asked.

Katy found herself stopped at the wall. She followed it to the corner where it met the wall of the house. The wall's top was a few inches over her head. She clutched the edge and tried to pull herself up, but it was impossible. She hopped again, making small whimpering noises. She was directly behind Grey's back. He turned to look at her, but relaxed when he saw there was no way she could clamber up. He called to her, but when she didn't come he turned back to Marcie, who was talking rapidly again.

Katy walked into the game room through the open doors. Grey was rising to get her when she appeared again. She carried one of her favorite toys, a ball almost as tall as she was, with a shag-carpet exterior. Katy dropped the ball and followed it as it rolled to the wall. Grey stayed on his feet.

"I went to college and law school at U.T." He and Marcie nodded with small smiles, acknowledging their academic kinship. "But I'm no longer functional as a lawyer. Temporarily retired from practice."

"Now, that in itself sounds criminal," Marcie said playfully. She had made only two or three random marks in her notebook. "You're much too young to retire. What are you, thirty- . . . ?"

". . . -four. But I said 'temporarily.' "

"You must have come into some money, and now you're taking time off. But doesn't that seem to you to correspond to the criminal's idea of making the big score and then quitting? They'll spend a lifetime looking for that, even if it fails every time, rather than pursuing a lifetime of honest work. Do you see that kind of attitude in your profession, lawyers looking for the one big case that will make them rich and famous?"

"Not that I've noticed," Grey said mildly. "I know it's a prevalent idea that criminal lawyers are just that, criminal. People think corporate lawyers sit around discussing the state of the economy while criminal lawyers talk about how to beat raps. Some lawyers even think that. But I don't think it means anything, it's just a result of the adversary nature of our judicial system. . . ."

Katy fell face-forward onto the shag ball, burying her face in its furry exterior and laughing. She looked up to see if this was getting the response it always did. Grey looked at her and smiled. Katy turned back to the ball. She couldn't roll over it as she usually did, because the ball was wedged in the corner.

"I really wanted to use a specific one of your cases as an example," Marcie said. Her eyes flicked past Grey to the baby in the corner, then back to the lawyer's face. A pale, earnest face, slightly globular, stuffed with too much concern. "You once had a client named Simon Hocksley." She glanced in her notebook. Grey frowned slightly. "Do you remember him?"

"Not offhand," Grey said, his eyes searching the hills at the horizon. "What was the case?"

"Robbery. It happened three years ago, just a few miles from here."

"Before we moved out here from town," Grey said absently. "Armed robbery?"

"Not exactly." Marcie was peering at him. Her pupils had become pinpoints in the sun, but they expanded slightly now with interest. "I believe there was originally an assault charge with the indictment, but that was dropped by the time it came to trial. He robbed that little grocery down on 271."

"Aauh." Grey made a noncommittal noise in his throat and began nodding. "Yeah. Hocksley. I remember. He had a jury trial."

"Uh-huh."

"I remember him," Grey said. "But there was nothing special about that case." He smiled. "Except that I lost it. What's your connection with it?"

"Nothing, really. I happened to be in court that day, with a friend who was contesting a speeding ticket." Grey cocked an eyebrow. Marcie's interest seemed more personal now. Her notebook had slipped off her knee and she didn't bother to pick it up. "I ran into somebody else I knew there—he happened to be there for the trial—so I watched some of it. And it's stuck with me for some reason. My first time in court, you know. And Simon Hocksley, he made a real impression on me. He was so scary-looking. Don't you remember him?"

"I remember him. But after you've been practicing for a while they don't leave much impression on you. Even the scary ones."

Marcie relaxed back into her chair and fanned herself with one hand. "You wouldn't believe it would get this hot in March, would you?" she said.

"I'm sorry, would you like something to drink? Coke or something?"

Marcie crossed her legs and smiled up at him. "That would be nice, Mr. Stanton."

"Grey."

"Grey. Kind of a funny name."

"My mother was a funny woman. I'll be right back. Katy."

Katy looked up from the ball but didn't move to follow him. As Grey hesitated Marcie said, "Oh, I'll watch her."

He looked from the baby to his guest. "Don't worry," Marcie said. He smiled slightly and stepped out of the sun. He hurried through the game room and down the stairs to the kitchen. While he got out ice and glasses he pictured the client in question, Simon Hocksley. A gruff, suspicious man who had had no defense to the charge but had expected as a matter of course that Grey would get him off. Grey had worked out what he thought was an eminently fair plea bargain, but Hocksley had insisted on a jury trial. When Grey had tried to warn him about the sentence he could receive from a jury, Hocksley had looked stubborn and said, "Let that woman sit in the same room with me and testify I done anything to her, with me watching her say it. I want to look at them people in the box and see them have the nerve to send me away." Grey had had little faith in his client's ability to scare people out of convicting him, but sure enough, when the trial came, the complaining witness had been evasive in her answers and Grey had managed to make her look like a liar. Still, the jury had known Simon was guilty of *some*thing. You could look at him and see that. Grey was afraid they'd try to give him a sentence of something like five hundred years. They had surprised him by coming back with a compromise sentence of eight years. Simon never realized how lightly he'd gotten off, though.

Grey hadn't thought like this in a while, analyzing a case, probing; even in memory he was planning strategy. It was nice to have an appreciative audience and he enjoyed talking to another adult. His world had become very narrow lately.

Upstairs on the terrace, Marcie paced lightly from her chair to the French doors. Katy buried her face in the shag of the ball again and looked at her hopefully, but Marcie wasn't watching. Katy gave up her quest for attention and looked from the ball to the top of the wall. She glanced again at Marcie, saw that she wasn't being watched, and reached for a hold in the shag.

After several false starts Katy managed to climb the ball. She put out a shaky hand and touched the top of the wall. With a tentative look of triumph she looked at Marcie. Marcie, standing near the doors, smiled at her and looked away. Katy stepped carefully from the ball to the top of the wall. The ledge there was a foot wide. As Katy put one foot on it, the other pushed off from the ball, which skittered away from the wall. In reaction Katy leaned too far forward, losing her precarious balance. For an instant she had a view of the faraway ground. She almost cried out then, but didn't, and a moment later she had both feet under her. She crouched on the ledge, her eyes blinking rapidly. The wind disarranged her thin blond strands of hair.

When Marcie heard Grey's foot on the stairs she called down, "So I remembered it, like I said, and that's why, when this paper idea came up, I thought I'd use that particular case. What I want to do is kind of compare the two of you, your attitude toward things."

Grey reached the top of the stairs, carrying glasses. "Ask away."

He came into the game room. Marcie was in the doorway to the terrace. He didn't see Katy, but saw Marcie look aside and smile.

"Mostly about violence," she said. "I think violence is the only real crime, don't you? I mean, I know there are others, but I just can't get very outraged over crimes against property, or moral codes, or, you know—"

"Well, I wouldn't want to write off all the other laws, but—"

"—you see what I mean. People hurting people is the worst thing. And Simon Hocksley was a violent man. He had a history of other assault-type crimes, even though he hadn't done time for any of them."

"You've really researched this, haven't you?" Grey said.

"He seemed like a man who had no compunction against using violence as a means to what he wanted," Marcie hurried on. She glanced aside again.

Grey was holding out a glass to her, but Marcie didn't take it. She was still in the doorway, blocking his way to the terrace.

"Aren't you scared of people like that?" she asked, changing tack. "I swear, just seeing him in court that one day made me—" She shivered. "He seemed so remorseless. Don't you—"

"You'd be surprised how docile they are after a night or a month in jail. Even the violent ones. I've never had any trouble."

Katy was standing on the ledge. It was really no harder than standing anywhere else, except the wind tickled her. She took a step, swayed a bit, and windmilled her arms to regain her balance. She still made no sound. Katy was a canny thirteen months. She knew that what she was doing was wrong, but she still hoped to elicit approval if she did it well enough. She wanted to make it all the way to the end of the wall and around the corner to where she'd be in Grey's sight again. She could hear his voice, talking to the stranger, who could see Katy clearly. Marcie directed a small smile at Katy that Katy took for approval. She beamed proudly and took another step.

Grey shook his head. "If you were that scared of your clients you'd have to get out of the business."

"But you are out of the business," Marcie said, smiling.

Grey laughed. "Well, yes, but not—"

A scream stopped him dead. The sound shot along Grey's nerves as if it had been conveyed telepathically, rather than traveling through the air. It drove him through the door and instinctively toward the last spot where he'd seen the baby. Later he would remember the little laugh he'd been laughing when he heard the scream. He would remember the split second he took to thrust the glasses toward Marcie before he dropped them. He would remember all the lost moments.

Katy was standing atop the wall. He swerved toward her, amazed at how much time he had. He was rushing headlong toward the baby, but before he had covered the short distance he had time to wonder how Katy had gotten up there, time to see the ball and figure it out, time to mentally lash himself for his stupidity.

He was seeing very clearly. He saw Katy's arms stretched toward him and saw her eyes lock on him as if that link could hold her up. Because Grey could also see very clearly that the baby was falling. She was moving in slow motion in relation to his spastically accelerated mental processes, but so was he. And the baby was falling.

The prolonged instant snapped. Time jerked forward again. By a stroke of luck Grey didn't deserve, the baby was falling *toward* him. He flung himself through the final separating feet of air and caught her as her feet left the top of the wall. He put out a hand to steady both of them, then held Katy to his chest with both arms. His eyes were closed in a moment of unworded prayer. When he opened them he saw Katy's face with the same startled look it had held as she started to fall off the wall. Grey forced himself to smile at her. She barely hesitated before smiling back.

The world was still enormously vivid. Katy's eyes were bluer than the sky at the top of the world. He looked over the wall and saw what his mind, working in a supplementary vein, had told him to expect. Judith was standing on the lawn looking up at him. She was absurdly foreshortened from this height, her feet bracketing her uplifted face. He could count the individual locks of her hair, blond but darker than the baby's. He could see her expression changing from terror to relief, and could read what expression would follow. A bag of groceries was spilled on the green, green lawn at Judith's feet. Another was still held in her left arm.

Judith finally unfroze and hurried into the house with the one bag of groceries. The other still lay on the lawn. Grey saw four oranges scattered on that terribly green grass, and couldn't think for a moment what they reminded him of: orange practice balls on a putting green. By the time he thought of it he had lost the intensity of his vision. The world receded from him again. Nothing was as vivid any more as the solid child in his arms.

Marcie had stepped out on the terrace. When he turned to her she picked up her purse and notebook from the chair. "I guess I'd better be going now. I would like to talk about this again sometime if you don't mind."

"Didn't you see her on the ledge?" Grey asked. He could feel Katy adding her stare to his own.

Marcie shrugged. "I didn't know she wasn't allowed up there. I guess I haven't had much experience with babies."

She made a wholly inadequate grimace—a "Silly me" expression—picked up her purse and notebook, and gave a small wave. Katy, fountain of forgiveness, waved back to her. Grey only nodded slightly and watched the girl step delicately through the glass doors and out of his sight. He thought about Judith and Marcie passing on the stairs, pictured the startled look Judith would give the girl, and wondered if they would take the time to introduce themselves.

# 2

GREY EMERGED FROM THE ACADEMIC CENTER, the undergraduate library at the University of Texas, with two books under his arm and a small smile of satisfaction on his face. He had scoured the library shelves on a dozen previous occasions, waiting for these two volumes to turn up, and today he had finally discovered both of them. He stopped for a moment at the top of the steps that led down to the west mall of the university. A man of medium height, his sandy hair beginning to fade away in front, Grey was in good shape, but that didn't come unconsciously, a right of birth, as it did to the young students all around him. What set Grey apart as well was that he took the time to look around. Everyone else in view was in a hurry. Undergraduate concerns are the most pressing in the world.

He left the campus, crossed Guadalupe, and

found his car in one of the crowded parking lots on the next street. As he dropped his books onto the front seat of the car, he stood in the sun a moment longer. The interior of the car was still cool, as if he'd carried into the city the atmosphere of his home. Grey was in no rush to return to that chill, and he realized suddenly he didn't have to do so. He was still unaccustomed to the relative leisure of his life. He had no appointments to keep, no schedule at all.

His law office was several blocks south of the university. After he drove past the state capitol and turned off the main commercial streets, the buildings he passed turned residential and their quality declined. The neighborhood was too familiar for Grey to notice its run-down character. It was that character that had allowed him and his partner to purchase their building cheaply enough that they could also afford the refurbishing necessary to turn it into a law office.

Grey parked at the curb and walked up the familiar sidewalk. Once a single-family home, then later broken down into apartments, the building had been sitting vacant when Grey and Harry had bought it, and the old house had been reincarnated into law offices. It was now a gallant anomaly, painted a stately dark gray and standing out from the surrounding rooming houses and apartments like the Queen Mother set down in a hobo jungle. Some clients thought the low-toned neighborhood would produce reduced rates. Other clients liked slipping in to see a lawyer whose office was not on the downtown streets.

It seemed to be the latter sort of clients who filled the waiting room today. Grey didn't recognize any of them, but that was hard to tell because they avoided his gaze as assiduously as massage-parlor customers. The exception was one elderly Mexican woman who raised her liquid, hopeful gaze to Grey and kept it on him as he moved to the receptionist's window.

Grey pressed most of his face into the round hole cut in the glass, but didn't speak until the receptionist raised her bored face from the typewriter. When she did she jumped back in her chair, shouted "Jesus Christ!" and clutched the vicinity of her heart. She kept her hand there long after she recognized Grey.

"What are you doing?" she asked indignantly. "Get in here."

Grey swam through the waiting Mexican woman's stare and through the door into Fran's office. She was standing now, still with her hand over her heart, until she threw both arms out to put them around Grey. Grey accepted the embrace, patting her back lightly. Fran was a tall woman, her long legs seeming to drive her higher than she really wanted to go, so that she was always bent at the knees or the waist. Their hug was quick and a little clumsy. When Fran pulled back Grey saw red everywhere. Her bright red lipstick was echoed only a bit more palely in her cheeks. Her hair, a slightly different shade of red every week, was long now and confined for the most part to the top of her head. She seemed to be leaning down to speak to Grey. Fran had never really mastered high heels. Each day she wore them seemed to be her first.

"What are you doing in this den of iniquity?" she said again, smiling through her mock outrage. "You better not be comin' back here. I told you you're not settin' foot in this place 'til you get that bestseller written."

Grey felt like a college boy embarrassed to be fussed over by an affectionate aunt. He put his hands in his pockets. "Looks like I'd get back just in time to have my name added to the indictments. What kind of fugitives are you harboring in that waiting room?"

"Aren't they terrible?" Fran didn't lower her voice one decibel. "That man's just let his criminal instincts spew all over the office since you left. I *swear* I'm gonna start carryin' a gun in here."

Grey smiled. Fran had been making this threat for years. "I noticed Harry's only keeping his own name dusted on the sign outside," he remarked untruthfully. The whole sign had been dusty.

"If I's you I'd come up here some dark night and cut my name *off* that sign. What're you gonna need with this crooked practice, anyway?"

Grey had given up trying to convince Fran that the legal history he was writing had no chance for wide sales. He stood with her for five more minutes, uncomfortably aware that Fran was ignoring the people in the waiting room while talking to him. "Is he in?" Grey finally asked.

"Probably back there doin' something nasty," Fran said. "You go on back and surprise him. Lemme know what you see when y' walk in."

Fran stood with her hands on her hips, shaking her head and smiling like a proud mother as Grey left the room. She was only four or five years his senior, but she had known him since his first day out of law school and had never given up the idea that she had raised him from a baby.

Against Fran's orders, Grey knocked on the door at the end of the dark hallway. Harry claimed that his clients felt comforted by meeting him at the end of thirty feet of shadows. Grey thought of the student who'd come to consult him, glad that she hadn't met Harry instead.

"Get the hell away from me, Fran!" the voice

came through the closed door. "I'll see one of those bastards when I'm good and goddamned ready!"

Grey opened the door. There was no indication that the man behind the desk had just been either loud or profane. He sat silently, apparently absorbed in the newspaper spread out on his desk. Harry was Grey's age, but his hair had started going gray as soon as he had entered private practice. It lightened his heavy face, which with its sun lines and beginnings of jowls looked closer to fifty than thirty-five. Grey had to admit that Harry's appearance made him look more important than Grey did. So would his clothes, if he had worn them properly. Today he had on his favorite three-piece gray pinstripe, but with a black shirt that clearly showed a sprinkling of ashes, as if a wind had blown the top layer of his suit across the shirt. His collar was open, his maroon tie wrapped around his powerful fist. A client might have thought he had cut his hand and wrapped it with the handiest cloth. Grey knew that Harry had removed the tie as soon as he'd returned from lunch, then absently wrapped it around his hand while reading the newspaper.

"So, Grey," Harry said without looking up, "you've come crawling back."

"Not yet." Grey stood in the doorway.

"Still got those delusions of grandeur? I think by now that should be grounds for commitment. You stay out another month, you asshole, and I'll have your whole half of the business laundered through Mexico and sitting in my account in Bermuda." Harry said it thoughtfully, as if he were really considering the plan and looking for Grey's opinion.

A conversation with Harry was an exercise in mutual belligerence. The better Harry liked a person, the ruder he treated him. He was polite only to judges and to men he intended to ruin.

"Looks like I'll be better off if you do," Grey said. "Fran tells me you've gone completely criminal in the short time I've been gone."

"Yeah." Harry still hadn't raised his eyes from the newspaper. "If you'll keep your goddamned liberal conscience out of here 'til the end of the year I'll be a millionaire."

Grey finally sat down, but left the door open. Harry closed it when he rose and crossed to the closet he used as a liquor cabinet.

"You know how many people are waiting to see you out there?" Grey asked.

Harry didn't interrupt his pouring to answer. Grey could have forgotten the reference by the time Harry handed him a glass and said, "Fuck 'em."

They drank to that toast.

It was twenty minutes and two drinks later when Harry cleared his throat and said, "So, uh, you just about ready to come back to work?" He moved papers on his desk, eyes down. Grey knew that it grated on Harry to ask a serious question. To cheer him up, Grey answered insultingly.

"Hell, Harry, I've only been gone a month. I guess it's hard for you to understand how long it takes to write a book, what with you never having read one."

Harry rolled his eyes.

"It might take a year, Harry. I told you that when I left."

"Yeah, yeah, yeah," Harry said grumpily.

"—unless you need me back here. Then of course I'd be glad to—"

"Oh hell," Harry said disgustedly. "Those two kids we hired are smarter than you and crookeder than me. You can *see* how damned busy I am."

"You haven't given one of them my office yet, have you?"

"Naw, we're just letting it fall into decrepitude before its time. Just like you."

"Gee, thanks."

Harry said sincerely, "I just hate to see you wasting your time. Losing your edge." He cleared his throat. "The truth is, Grey, I'm afraid that by the time you do come back you won't be worth shit any more but I'll have to keep you on for old times' sake."

"I'm touched by your concern," Grey said.

"Yeah, I'm a sentimental guy."

Fran was on the phone when Grey left. She

waved to him with a casualness that assumed he'd be back soon. Grey was glad to see, on his way through the waiting room, that the old Mexican woman had gotten in to see someone. He realized as he went out the door that he wished it were him she had come to see. He missed the everyday life of the office.

The sun glared in his eyes as he drove west, toward home. Grey put on sunglasses, he lowered his visor, but the sun kept levering itself down, creeping under the visor's protection, reminding him of the time. He was running later than he should have been.

He left his window open to the warm day, hoping it would clear his head and dispel the fumes of Harry's whiskey. He couldn't smell it, but Judith might. There was nothing wrong with a couple of drinks in the afternoon with an old friend, but Grey felt particularly vulnerable to criticism now. He knew his wife's nature. Her forgiveness would not come in a gush. It would come trickling in for a long time; he'd never know when he had the full amount. And any further lapse of responsibility on his part would halt the flow.

Fifteen miles outside Austin he turned off the two-lane highway. After more than a year it still seemed new to him to be alone on the road when he was almost home. They had no neighbors here, had made no new friends. They owned only the acre on which the house was set, but their nearest neighbor was two miles away. Grey parked behind the house, leaving it deserted-looking from the road.

Katy ran to meet him when he came in the kitchen door. He picked her up and hugged her, but kept his face averted. Don't kiss the baby with liquor on your breath: she'll grow up to be an alcoholic. Since becoming a father Grey had grown susceptible to old wives' tales, even ones he had invented himself. Katy squealed, telling him something without bothering to fit in the words she knew. "I see," Grey said anyway.

Judith was standing in the hall doorway. Katy had forgotten the ledge, but Judith hadn't. She had hardly let Katy out of her sight in the days since, even when Grey was there to watch her.

"Hi," he said.

"Get everything done?" There was no tension in the way Judith leaned on the doorframe. She wasn't nervous, just watchful.

"Pretty much. Stopped by the office on the way back. Everyone said to say hi. Hi."

He set Katy down, and she went out of the kitchen ahead of them. When Grey didn't come quickly enough, Katy came back for him and gripped his pants leg, using it for support while steering him into the living room. Grey and Judith smiled at each other. "Has she been all right?" he asked.

"Not too bad. She took a nap. So did her mother, almost."

"You're getting lazy. You'll never be able to go back to work."

"Ha ha ha," Judith said. They both knew how much chance for laziness there was around Katy.

"I'm going to take a shower," Grey announced. Katy had released him. She started to follow him up the stairs, but Judith took her. Grey heard the baby start to cry, then stop almost immediately as Judith distracted her with something.

Grey had lied to Judith about the baby's walk on the ledge. He had told Judith that he'd been right there beside her, holding her hand; Judith's angle of vision had prevented her seeing him. It had been an instinctive lie. The circumstances were just too damning: Grey talking to some strange young woman while his daughter almost fell off the roof. He knew how negligent he'd been, he'd spent the days since mentally lacerating himself. But Grey knew it would never happen again. The fear had imprinted itself on him too strongly. Judith had no such assurance. He'd lied as much to ensure her peace of mind as to protect himself.

Judith was skeptical, but she went along with the story. They had to be tender of each other's feelings now because they were together constantly. It was still surprising to see each other at home during weekdays. When they first met they had both worked. Grey had just moved from a large firm to his private practice with Harry. Judith was a loan officer. Her bank, on the strength of Judith's opinion, had declined to give the young lawyers a loan. Judith thought they needed more experience. Harry had gotten the loan elsewhere, but by that time Grey and Judith had taken their discussions out of the bank and out of the realm of finance. Harry claimed Grey had married her in order to have a corner on her business sense, which was formidable.

Judith had found much to criticize at her own bank and other offices around town, from the way records were kept to the decor. She planned to start her own business, though her plans were still a little unfocused. She had begun to lean toward specializing in furnishing executive suites. But there was plenty of time for Judith to define her plans. She wouldn't start until Katy was old enough.

Grey had no doubt she would succeed. She always had. Without using her womanhood to advantage, Judith was everyone's equal. Grey had once hoped to impress her by taking her to a reception at the governor's mansion. Grey introduced Judith to the attorney general, then to a justice of the Texas supreme court, and was proud to see her hold her own. But somewhere he lost control of the evening. Both of them were introduced to the governor's wife, a slightly flustered woman new to public life. Judith was very gracious, putting her own hostess at ease. When they were introduced to their host Judith and the governor soon discovered an old school connection through her father. The governor had taken her in tow like a favorite daughter, and when his wife had retired early with a headache, Judith had taken over as hostess. When she and Grey left the party, the governor warned Grey that he might have to appropriate Judith again on some official occasion.

On the other hand, Grey had seen Judith stand nose to nose with an angry, sweating lumberyard owner and explain to him just how he had screwed up his business to the point that the bank couldn't loan him any more money. With no change in her careful vocabulary, she had seemed to answer him curse for curse, and the man had left promising to make changes. Grey had been impressed with Judith's serenity under pressure.

She had stopped working after they'd finally decided the time was right to have a baby. Judith had been over thirty at the time, and the decision meant for her a long commitment. Once she was pregnant she'd had an amniocentesis to be sure the baby would be healthy.

She quit her job in the eighth month of her pregnancy, and wasn't planning to go back to work until Katy started school. She was throwing herself into motherhood with the same single-mindedness she brought to the rest of her life.

Judith was not cold, but she was controlled. Grey was under the impression that she had in her mind a numbered list of priorities. Right now the baby came first. Then Grey, then her ambition to own a business. Grey sometimes feared that if he did something too terrible or stupid he'd actually be able to see himself sliding down a notch on her list.

If Judith was deferring her ambitions for the moment, Grey was finally fulfilling his. Since law school he'd had a book in mind, a history of the jury system. During the ten years since, he'd been saving money to trade for time. He'd had to put it off when they'd bought this house, put it off again when they decided to have Katy. But the time had finally come when he knew if he delayed any longer, he'd delay for the rest of his life. He had the money now to take the time to write the book: a year if they were very careful, six months if the savings kept dwindling at the rate they were now.

Judith was cooking when he emerged from the shower. Grey sniffed, dressed hurriedly, and went downstairs to take the spoon from her hand. He took up the stirring duties.

"Not too much," she said, her thanks implicit.

They ate with Katy between them, encouraging her to mimic their use of silverware. She was coming along well, but was still enough of a failure that it was a gallant gesture of Grey's to clean up after her when they finished. It wasn't his turn. "Thank you," Judith said, then to Katy, "Say thank you. Thank you." She sat with the baby on her lap until Grey finished and they all went into the living room.

Grey took charge of Katy until her bedtime, and was happy to see that Judith didn't look up every time the baby made a sudden noise.

"What are you reading?" he asked, to start a conversation.

"Catalog." Judith showed him facing pictures of leather sofas.

"That doesn't look like office furniture."

"If you try to make your office look like an office," Judith said automatically, "it will look like everyone else's office."

Judith looked up to see Grey smiling. He'd heard the line before. "Sorry," she said, smiling as well. "Giving you my sales pitch again."

Until they got Katy to sleep, the conversation centered around the baby. Afterward Grey told Judith more about his visit to the office. "By the time I go back the firm's reputation may be so unsavory I won't want to rejoin it."

Judith smiled at the exaggeration. "Speaking

of crooked lawyers, that girl called you today." To Grey's uncertain look she amplified: "The student interviewer."

"Oh," Grey said, consciously trying to look uninterested. Mention of Marcie made him feel guilty because she was a reminder of the near-tragedy of Katy on the ledge. He certainly didn't want Judith to think he'd neglected his daughter because he'd been too attentive to the young, attractive woman.

Judith didn't lose her smile as she watched his face reflect this thought process. "Say something innocuous about her," she said with gentle mockery.

"What did she say?"

"Just that she wanted to talk to you. She didn't want to talk to me," she added.

"Of course not. You're not the subject of her thesis."

Judith came and sat beside him on the couch. "Don't look so uncomfortable." Grey's discomfiture made her indulgent. She put a hand on his leg with the most warmth she'd shown him in days.

"I'm glad you're so transparent," Judith said.

"Uh—"

"If you ever have an affair, I'll know the second I see your face."

"Oh yeah? You've never caught me yet."

"Ha ha ha," Judith said again, leaning into him.

# 3

MARCIE WAS AN INTRUSION ON THE FRAGILE SIlence. Her call early in the afternoon had brought Katy upright in Judith's lap just as the baby was dropping into her post-lunch nap. It had taken half an hour to get her asleep again. Now Marcie was here in person and her voice was louder than the telephone's ring had been. She didn't seem to notice how quiet the Stantons kept their own voices and footsteps. She didn't know the house, couldn't see the invisible lines that carried every sound straight up to Katy's sleeping ears. The nursery was the first room at the top of the stairs, and the foot of the stairs came directly down into the living room.

Marcie stood and wandered across the room, stopping at the bookcase beneath the stairs. Grey and Judith followed, staying close to her, but she still raised her voice as if she'd left them on the far side of the room. "You don't keep any law books here?"

Judith looked up, following that question straight up the shaft of the stairwell. Grey glanced at her and her eyes came down to his.

"Not out here," he answered. "I have a few in my study. Why don't we go in there and talk?"

"I'll go up and check on the baby," Judith said pointedly.

She started up the stairs as Grey motioned Marcie around them. His study was behind the living room and across a short hallway. The study shared the back wall of the house with the kitchen, a larger room only a few steps down that hall. If you left the study and walked past the kitchen doorway a step or two, the hall turned right and ran straight to the front door, past the archway into the living room. It was a small house, only three rooms downstairs and three up. Judith was already at the top of the stairs when she heard the study door close. The nursery was on her left. She stood in the doorway and looked at the baby, still sleeping. The nursery was directly over the study, but she could no longer hear Marcie's voice. Judith looked down the upstairs hallway. The door of the master bedroom, on the same wall as the nursery, was closed, and catercorner to it was the open door of the game room, which opened out onto the terrace. Judith thought the terrace doors might be open and went to check.

Grey ushered Marcie into his study and closed the door. The study was a small room, so her voice would seem even louder, but the shelves of books exerted a muffling influence. Grey sat at the desk, watching impatiently as Marcie examined the books in this room as well. "Would you like something to drink?" he finally said.

Turning, she said, to his slight annoyance, "Yes."

"Tea? Or wine. Or I think there's—"

"Wine would be nice." She smiled at him.

Grey left her studying the books, closed the door behind him, and walked the few steps to the kitchen doorway on his left. Judith was in the kitchen sipping iced tea, her face neutral. It was extraordinary the way she could watch someone with her face perfectly bare of expression. Grey grimaced, and the blank surface of her face returned a hastily departing reflection of that expression. As he poured from the bottle in the refrigerator he said, "Why don't you join us?"

"No thanks. I'd better stay out here and listen for Katy."

"I'll try to get rid of her." Carrying the two wineglasses, he brushed Judith's cheek with his lips. He had a feeling the forgiveness process, which had been proceeding so smoothly, had come to a halt with Marcie's reappearance.

Back inside the study, he pushed the door

closed with his foot. Marcie must have heard the sound, but didn't turn. Grey stood behind her holding the two glasses of wine. When he cleared his throat the girl stepped back, almost stepping into him as she turned and put out a hand. He took a hasty step back himself, holding the glasses away in fear she would spill them. Marcie's hand came to rest on his chest, just as her eyes caught up to her body's movement.

"Oh." They both chuckled and apologized. Grey handed her one of the glasses and retreated to his desk chair again. "I don't know how much more I can do for you. Still interested in that one case we talked about?"

"Uh-huh." Marcie took the seat across from him, sipped her wine, and nodded her thanks. "I think it's going to be a really good paper."

"Maybe you should check with my office in town. They'd have the records." Grey had no qualms about palming Marcie off on Harry and Fran. They wouldn't let her impose on them.

"I did that. I talked to Mr. Harrison."

"Really. You are industrious. Was he helpful?"

"He . . . would have . . . liked to be." Her phrasing was delicate, each word apparently picked from a score of harsher ones she could have used. "But of course he's a busy man and his time isn't free."

Great. She comes to ask about a case and

Harry tries to proposition her. "I'm sorry," Grey said sincerely. "I'm sure he didn't mean to—"

"Oh no, that's all right. Nothing for you to apologize about."

A moment's awkward silence. Marcie's eyes met his and slid away again. Grey sat in a welter of embarrassment, feeling responsible for his partner, his profession, the sorry state of the world.

Marcie's gaze found her open notebook. "Oh." Hastily reading a note, she said, "Did Mr. Hocksley have any partners in the robbery?"

"Not that I ever heard about."

"Did it seem like a spontaneous sort of crime, or something he had planned out? And if he did have a partner, couldn't he have gotten a lighter sentence if he'd turned that person in?"

"Possibly," Grey said. He described the plea-bargaining process at some length, grateful to have the formal questions and answers passing between them. Their eyes could hold on each other now. Marcie smiled slightly at her complicity in this plot to escape their mutual embarrassment. Behind the smokescreen of his serious words, Grey smiled back.

By the end of their session Grey was no longer irritated at her visit. It was nice to talk about a subject with which he was familiar, and watch Marcie make studious notes. It was much easier than picking his way through the intricacies of the history he was trying to write. He felt he'd concluded a job well done when Marcie closed her notebook, rose, and extended her hand. "It was very kind of you to talk to me again," she said. "I hope you'll let me bother you once or twice more if I have new questions."

Grey rose slowly and took the hand she offered. "Couldn't we answer them now?"

"I don't know what they'd be at the moment," Marcie said apologetically. "I just thought something might come up after I talk to Mr. Hocksley."

Grey showed his surprise. "You are serious about this, aren't you? Won't that be a lot of trouble?"

"Not too much."

"A trip to Huntsville?"

"Oh, I thought you knew. Simon Hocksley is getting out today. He lives just a few miles from here."

Simon Hocksley looked to be in his element. His boots, laced halfway up his calves, were crusted with years-old mud. The broken brim of his slouch hat fell down over his eyes. He was pale, but in his dark clothes the shadows accepted him readily. He emerged from the shed in his front yard carrying a pick and a shovel.

His other implement was a pistol shoved down in his waistband.

Simon Hocksley was between thirty-five and forty-five, with black, bristling hair and eyes encircled by deep wrinkles. The eyes looked secretly amused, captives who knew their own power. In contrast to his pale skin, the eyes with their wrinkles suggested years in the sun. Simon was a thin man, honed down to essentials, strong-looking. Tendons moved clearly under the skin of his forearm. The arm suggested the inner workings of a piano. He shifted his grip on his tools, striking a new chord beneath his skin.

He looked around the yard, sending his final glare through a window of the house. Nothing showed there. The house, added on to a few times by inexpert carpenters, looked like a crowd of casual strangers wondering what had brought them together. It was more than a mile from the nearest road, with only a rutted track leading in. There was enough daylight left for Simon to be sure he was unobserved when he entered the woods.

Half an hour later he was deeper into the trees and into the evening. Still glaring around suspiciously, more so now that darkness had closed him in, he finally convinced himself that he hadn't been followed. He stood beside a blasted stump, its hollow water-filled. Dropping the pick and shovel from his shoulder, he carried one in each hand as he carefully marked the direction and struck off at a new angle. Ten minutes brought him to his last landmark. He found the tree, laid a hand on its bark, and studied the ground for signs of disturbance. Then he stood rigid, straining his senses, until suddenly he dropped the shovel and in the same motion brought the pick over and down. It bit strongly into the moist earth at the base of the tree.

Simon dug quickly, switching from pick to shovel to pick and occasionally to pistol, standing in the hole with the gun drawn. But as he got deeper he became less cautious, until he laid the pistol on the ground and forgot it. He was thigh-deep in the hole by then, each new thrust with the pick or the shovel a cautious one followed by a slight pause. That phase passed too. Soon he was striking blindly downward with the pick, hitting as many spots as he could, not bothering to clear the hole of the ruptured dirt. When it got too full he dropped to his knees and dug with his hands. His nails filled with embedded dirt, they cracked and broke off; dirt filled the network of cracks in his hands until his veins seemed to be carrying black blood. He flung the dirt about haphazardly, often covering his back or stomach or arms. His knees sank deeper into the loam.

He didn't stop until he had dug a shallow

moat around the tree. Fury carried him around and around the tree, his tools taking him deeper into the empty earth, until he tripped on a root and fell face-forward into the hole. He lay there exhausted, stretching his arms out, pushing his fingers down like roots of his own.

When he had recovered he climbed wearily out of his trench and studied the tree. His attention traveled closely from the roots to the branches above his head. He circled the tree, slipping back down into the hole a couple of times. Finally he stood with his back to the tree, looking around at its companions. He hurried back through the woods, found his marks, and retraced his route. It brought him to the same tree.

Anger took him again, dispelling the uncertainty. He snatched up the pick on the run and slammed it into the ground at the base of another tree. Demented, he struck the earth again and again, gouging out chunks of dirt, growling inarticulately whenever the pick stuck for an instant.

Waylon Hocksley waited in the house. Four years younger than Simon, he was more powerfully built and less restless. He was alone in the house, in the only lighted room, his consciousness totally indrawn. A black-and-white TV flickered in front of him. Its picture slipped, lost its hold, and began flipping steadily upward. It was a long minute before the movement caught Waylon's attention. He rolled forward and kicked the side of the set, knocking the rabbit ears to the floor on the other side.

Waylon sat in the wheelchair that had been rescued from a scrap yard without consulting its owner. He sometimes wondered who had thrown the thing away. What confidence, to discard a working wheelchair. Waylon thought it might have been a sign of the passage of a faith healer. More likely it evidenced a cripple's death. The chair seemed to have no miraculous properties.

Without turning his head, Waylon rolled himself backward in a tight semicircle to the other side of the TV set. He picked up the rabbit ears and was adjusting them on top of the set when the front door opened. Waylon heard it, and felt the breeze on the back of his neck, but got the picture adjusted before he turned to look.

Simon looked like a creature escaped from a grave. He could have been no more filthy if he'd been buried for years and had just clawed his way up into the air tonight. He had been digging for hours. Dirt still sifted free and fell from his hair and face and shoulders. A black aura surrounded him. "Waylon!" he said loudly.

His brother had rolled forward after he turned, but stopped at the sound of his name. He made no answer, just watched the creature in the doorway. Simon's eyes, the only unblackened spots in his face, burned toward Waylon. Waylon sat limply, his expression dead.

"Where's my money?" Simon said. His voice was low, impatient, the voice of a man who has already been through long preliminaries of talk.

Waylon said nothing, knowing any answer would be useless. Simon advanced on him.

"The money I got from the store. It's not where I left it."

They just stared at each other until Simon lost his patience and loudly slapped Waylon's face. "Goddamn it, Waylon, I did three years for that money! You took it!" Waylon was shaking his head. "You took it!" Simon said again.

Simon was leaning down with his hands on the armrests of the wheelchair. He stood again, put his muddy boot on one armrest, and pushed. The chair lurched backward across the floor, Waylon swinging his arms for balance. One of the wheels caught on a chair leg and the wheelchair went over backward, spilling Waylon to the floor. He lay there on his elbows.

"I didn't take it."

"You must have," Simon said. He was tired. His voice carried no conviction. "I didn't tell anyone else."

"Damn it, Simon, you didn't tell *me!* Try to remember. You think I'd still be here, waiting for you, if I'd taken the money?"

Simon swayed, finally slumped into a frayed armchair. "I must have told you," he said quietly.

"You didn't." Waylon pushed himself up onto the sofa. "You know you didn't."

Simon rubbed his eyes. "I went to jail for it," he said, almost whimpering from fatigue. "They owe me the money." A sudden surge of energy lifted him to his feet, facing his brother. "*You* owe it to me!"

Waylon just stared at him. Simon's fit of energy passed as quickly as it had appeared. When his shoulders slumped, Waylon said, "You must have told someone else. Was anyone with you when you hid it?"

"Of course not."

Waylon pressed. "Someone else had to know. Who else knew you had it? Someone you were in jail with?"

Simon shook his head. His eyes roved blindly around the room. He couldn't remember anything.

"What about your lawyer?" Waylon finally said.

"My lawyer?"

"Didn't you tell him all about the case? Maybe he even did some investigating on his own."

"My lawyer." The energy level was rising in Simon's voice again. "I told him I'd pay him some of the money if he got me off."

"He didn't," Waylon said shortly. "You didn't tell him where the money was?"

Simon's eyes went sideways, his memory backward. "I must have," he finally said. "He must've found out."

They looked at each other across the dim room.

# 4

GREY RAISED HIS HEAD AS SUDDENLY AS IF HE'D heard a door slam. None had. He was alone in the house, working in his study. The door that had slammed was in his mind. It severed all contact with his work. One moment he was working well, as he had been all morning and early afternoon. The next moment he couldn't remember what he'd been thinking. His book seemed like one he'd read years ago and forgotten.

For long minutes Grey struggled to finish the sentence he'd started, then gave it up. He had already done a good day's work, and any further effort would be wasted. He tossed his pen to the desk.

Stretching his arms seemed to accentuate his aloneness, enlarge all the room he had to himself. Judith had gone into Austin for lunch and shopping. Things were almost perfectly easy between them again, but Judith had still taken Katy with her, saying she was going to drop in on her mother, who would consider the visit wasted if it didn't include an appearance by her granddaughter. Grey thought it was an excuse not to leave Katy in his care, but he was just as glad to be left alone. His legal history was going slowly.

But now that he was finished with it for the day, the emptiness of the house pressed in on him. He felt lazy and unproductive. When he was in the office he didn't consider time spent chatting or reading newspapers wasted, but when he was at home the instant he stopped working he was a bum.

Presently his emptiness expressed itself as hunger. He went to the kitchen looking for something to gnaw. The kitchen, dominated by a huge window above the sinks, was awash in sunshine. Grey was drawn past the refrigerator to the view behind the house. The pool winked at him.

It was an extravagance. They would never have built one themselves, but it had come with the house. Oh well, they'd said, since it's already here . . . and Katy can learn to swim. In reality, they had only taken her in a few times, and though the baby loved the water, her parents were scared to death of that attraction.

Grey wandered outside, his snack forgotten. Hands in pockets, he tipped his face up to the sun. The day was very warm, probably ninety degrees. Grey looked down into the pool. His vision floated on its surface as he could imagine his body doing. The water was fairly clean. He had filled the pool during that January warm spell that had fooled the trees into putting forth their first premature buds, but they'd had another freezing spell before he could use it. The fresh water was still virgin.

It would be silly to go in. The day was warm, but the water would still be cold. Its brightness was a lure for fools. He crouched to stick a hand in the water. It wasn't as cold as he had expected, but only an idiot would judge by the surface temperature. He told himself that all the way back inside and up the stairs. By the time he had looked through three drawers and two closet shelves to find his trunks he had stopped kidding himself that he just wanted to see if they fit.

He hit the water with a running splash, then forced himself to slide further into the depths. His discipline gave out before he reached the bottom, and he came clawing his way out, gasping and shouting and almost, for an instant, managing to stand atop the water.

Yes, the water was too cold. The sun, though, was warm. Grey found one of their inflatable rafts, blew it up while standing in the shallow end, and carefully eased himself aboard.

That was the perfect compromise. The sun

lulled him, the occasional splash of cold water kept him conscious. He lay on his back, the sun turning the insides of his eyelids into a pyrotechnic theater. His pulse entered the raft and the water and his eardrums until the whole world moved to that slow beat. His skin warmed, dried, sought and found that perfect temperature that all life seeks. Time lost its dominance.

"This is just where I was hoping to find you!"

Grey was startled into alertness and guilt. Judith's was the only voice he could have expected, and with air slowly seeping out of the raft his head had become half-submerged, so he hadn't heard the voice at all, only its vibrations through the water. The answer he framed was to his wife: "I already worked for hours, I didn't just jump in as soon as you—"

The answering laugh was not Judith's. Grey opened his eyes into the sun, closed them again, shaded his face with his hand. He had lost track of where he was in the pool. He was next to the side farther from the house. He pushed off from it toward the opposite side, where Marcie, the student interviewer, stood looking down at him.

"What a guilty conscience you must have." She grinned. Marcie was dressed for the warm weather in cut-off jeans and a white Mexican peasant blouse with some kind of pattern picked out in blue and red thread. Her feet were bare and her legs were longer than Grey had realized.

"Hello," he said. He tried leaning up and resting on his elbows, but the air mattress gave under the pressure so that his head was no higher than it had been. "You startled me."

"I'm sorry," she said lightly. "Thinking about your work?"

His air mattress was still drifting slowly toward her, and the closer he came the more dominating a figure she seemed, standing above him with her hands on her hips, looking approvingly at the surrounding hills.

"I don't think I was thinking at all," he said. "Just floating."

She nodded. "I know. It's that kind of day. To tell you the truth, I was hoping to find you in the pool."

Abruptly she grasped the hem of her blouse and pulled it off over her head. Dropping her blouse to the concrete apron of the pool, she unzipped her shorts and let them fall as well. "You can see what I came for."

Noticing Grey's stare, she suddenly sounded less confident. "I hope it's all right. I'm sorry, I should have—"

Under her clothes she was wearing a purplish bikini. "No, it's fine," Grey said. He felt obliged to be a good host even though she had forced the duty on him. "Really, I'm glad of the company. It gets lonely out here in the sticks."

"You're just being polite," Marcie said accurately, "but luckily I'm willing to take advantage of you." She looked down at herself and pulled a hand across her stomach. "God knows I need to get some sun."

Grey refrained from comment. It was true her flesh was pale, but that was the only thing wrong with it. Her stomach was flat and showed the attention of exercise. Out of her clothes she seemed firmer and more substantial. Grey was surprised by the size of her breasts, which her blouse had disguised but which the bikini top covered only half-attentively. Grey slid off the air mattress into the cold water.

"Cold?" Marcie asked when he gasped slightly. He nodded vigorously. "Oh, it can't be that cold. Let's see."

She leaped high and entered the pool in a smooth dive close to where he was treading water. Grey backstroked away from the splash, toward the shallow end, and watched her through the intervening water. For a moment Marcie's progress toward the bottom of the pool was smooth and graceful, but then he saw the coldness of the water hit her. She turned, kicking and stroking and rising rapidly through the water until she came clawing her way out of it. Her hands reached and clutched convulsively, seeking a purchase on the sunlight as she tried futilely to climb completely out of the water.

She fell back in, then scrambled toward where he stood in the shallows. Her teeth were clenched and she was rubbing her arms frantically.

"It's freeeeezing!" she shrieked, sounding like a little girl. Grey couldn't help laughing. Marcie didn't stop until she was standing very close in front of him. For just a moment she stayed there, but before it became awkward for him she stepped back, gliding into slightly deeper water. She spread her arms and put her head back, exposing as much skin as she could to the sun. Her bikini top was doing its job even less efficiently now that it was wet. Grey's gaze slipped downward from her closed eyes. After a moment he retrieved the raft and rested his arms on it, the raft between their bodies.

"Have you seen Mr. Hocksley yet?" he asked.

"Who? Oh. No. I didn't come about the paper, really. I did have some general questions about law school, because I'm doing some applications now. But mostly I just wanted to get out of town. I'm sorry," she apologized again.

Grey felt suspicious and flattered. A pretty girl, a student, there must have been plenty of places she could have gone rather than see him. She was probably angling for a letter of recommendation to his old law school. You need recommendations from established lawyers when you apply, he remembered. It wasn't much of a favor to ask, and Grey was inclined to be indulgent. He wasn't so old, he told himself, that he didn't know what it was to need help.

Just as he was about to ask if that was what she wanted, Marcie let herself fall back, turned when she was underwater, and glided away from him in long, slow strokes of her legs and arms. She was probably too embarrassed to ask immediately, Grey thought. He began swimming himself. The coldness of the water encouraged activity. Marcie turned at the far wall of the pool, still underwater, and started back. Their paths crossed somewhere in the middle, and Grey saw her eyes open as his shadow passed over her. She came up beside him, barely out of breath, and matched his pace to the far edge of the pool. When Grey pulled slightly ahead she smiled challengingly and swam faster herself. They were neck and neck when they reached the wall, and by unspoken agreement they turned, kicked off, and raced to the shallow end. They bumped each other once but then straightened out their courses and pulled through the water as hard as they could.

Grey was a strong swimmer and was surprised to find Marcie keeping up with him. Somewhere over halfway he lost his rhythm and was flailing at the water much too hard. Marcie's smooth strokes never faltered. He felt like a steamboat beside a dolphin, but in the end he beat her to the far side by about three feet.

Marcie laughed loudly and jumped up out of the water. The purple bikini didn't quite keep up, but she didn't seem to notice. She was as exuberant as a child. "Pretty good!" she shouted. She calmed down somewhat and stood next to him. Grey was leaning back, arms outstretched on the side of the pool as he breathed deeply. Marcie didn't seem winded.

"I was on the swimming team in high school," she said. "I was sure I could beat you. You're in better shape than I thought."

"—for an old man," Grey said, but she ignored it. She was looking at him thoughtfully.

"And you know, you don't look nearly so—um—scholarly in a bathing suit." When he laughed she shook her head, realizing she had embarrassed him. "You know what I mean," she said quickly. "Come on!"

She dived back into the water and after a moment Grey followed her. They stayed active in the water for a while, swimming another couple of races, playing tag underwater, playful as children. There was a moment or two when their play didn't seem innocent to Grey, but he didn't think Marcie shared that feeling. He was getting too old and cynical, he decided. In their games some occasional brushings of their bodies were inevitable, and once Marcie even threw her arms around his neck and their bodies pressed together full length, but it only lasted for a moment and she was laughing the whole time, so it wasn't exactly erotic. But it did make him thoughtful.

Grey rested in the shallow end after a while, but Marcie didn't seem tired. She swam to one of the ladders and pulled herself out, her back to him. The bottom of the bikini was a trifle too large, too.

She hopped onto the diving board and bounced on it experimentally. Then she stood still and put a hand to her breast, acknowledging for the first time the provocativeness of what she was wearing. "This is my roommate's suit. She's a little—" Her hands described an arc of breasts larger than her own.

Grey was wise enough not to offer any of the responses that sprang to mind. "That's okay," he finally said lamely.

"For *her.*" Marcie grinned. She bounced again, then once more, and finally the highest yet, and leaped high off the board. She entered the water smoothly, her momentum barely slowed, and knifed toward where Grey stood near the middle of the pool. He watched her body, smooth as the water itself, stretching toward him and displayed as if under glass. Her entry into the water had tugged her bikini bottom a couple of indiscreet inches down her hips. He stared at her and realized he had almost forgotten this feeling. Marriage hadn't killed his imagination, it just had made his imaginings remote. In fact, it had made looking at other women more pleasant, because there was nothing to it but appreciativeness. This was different. Being barely clothed in the water with Marcie gave his speculations an inescapable immediacy. What he had forgotten was the nervous but heady quality of such speculation, like a first date.

She swam past him underwater, her leg brushing his. It could have been an invitation, and for a moment he was willing to accept it. His thoughts surprised him. He had never been unfaithful to Judith, in fact the possibility had seemed unlikely to the point of nonexistence. It still was, he told himself; this was just a summerish fantasy. But it was more realistic than any other fantasy he'd ever had. It would be so easy here in the pool, her bikini already slipping off—

Marcie rose out of the water and climbed the steps in the shallow end. Grey continued to stare as her fingers came down to adjust her bikini bottom, but then her hands stopped on her hips and when he looked up she was staring back at him. Neither of them looked away and neither wore much expression. Marcie's gaze was flat, not coy or even inquisitive. The power of her direct look was disconcerting. Grey was certain she was reading his mind. But what she read was only the desire, not the restrictions and rationalizations that hedged it.

It turned into one of those moments that last

too long, until it seems nothing could end it. Grey finally lowered his eyes and made small sweeping motions with his hands in the water. "Well," he said lamely, "didn't you come to talk about law school?"

Even that innocuous remark was the wrong thing to say, he saw when he looked back at her. Her expression had turned slightly contemptuous, and he realized she thought he was bargaining with her, offering an exchange of favors. He looked down again and shook his head, but that wouldn't be enough to dislodge her unspoken assumption. Nor could he try to convince her it had been a harmless remark. To say "I didn't mean it that way" would only be to acknowledge that such a meaning *had* occurred to him.

Giving up, he sank back into the water and swam toward the other end. The only thing he could do to correct the impression she had of him now was simply to stay away from her and act as if he expected nothing. But when he came up on the far side of the pool he saw her walking toward him along the edge. She still looked knowing, but no longer angry. She had a small smile, in fact. She had decided to accept the bargain. She dived into the water and came slowly toward him.

They swam races again and Marcie enticed him into a game of tag in which he halfheartedly joined, but there was no longer anything playful or childlike about her. That same knowing look was never far from her expression. It was clear that she thought the balance of obligation had shifted in her favor. She had come here asking for Grey's help but now it was he who owed her.

She seemed to be enjoying herself. Only Grey felt guilty. He had given her this false impression because it wasn't entirely false. He was to blame. Grey suddenly thought of the picture he and Marcie would present, frolicking in the water, if Judith returned at this moment. Even as much as his wife trusted him, she could be forgiven for thinking the same thing Marcie was thinking, especially when she saw the look on Marcie's face. He felt responsible to everyone.

Grey climbed out of the pool. He thought about going inside, getting dressed, and disclaiming all connection with Marcie. Dear? Judith would say. There seems to be a half-naked girl in our pool. Really? I wonder where she could have come from.

He was sitting in a lawn chair sometime later and Marcie was still in the water near his feet, her arms and head resting on the edge as she asked him some very general questions about law school. When he did hear the crunch of tires on the gravel of the driveway, he almost levitated to his feet. If Judith pulled all the way around to the back she would be almost on top of them in seconds. Grey's guilt came surging back. Probably Judith would view the scene more innocently than he was imagining because she couldn't read his thoughts, but on the other hand he was never sure she couldn't.

"That will be Judith," he said, hoping to stir Marcie out of the pool and into more clothing.

She smiled at him with a certain intimacy and shrugged as if their chance were gone.

When the back door of the house opened he called loudly, "Hello," and stood up. Judith came toward him, looking cool and proper in a pale green dress. Her pleasant expression didn't change when she glanced past Grey. She had already taken in Marcie's presence. She could also see her clothes on the apron of the pool, and from Judith's angle she could only see Marcie's head and shoulders.

"Get much done today?" she asked Grey as she drew closer.

Her tone sounded ironic. Grey resisted the inclination to look down at Marcie. Instead he walked to meet Judith, and touched her arm lightly. She was looking past him. "Hello," she said.

Marcie waved to her. "Hi. Hope you don't mind."

"Of course not." Judith smiled at her again before turning to Grey. Her eyes seemed to probe his conscience. Under the circumstances, no expression of hers would have looked unsuspicious to Grey.

"I did get a lot of work done earlier," he said hurriedly. "But it was such a nice day. I was already in the pool when Miss . . . when Marcie arrived."

"More questions?" Judith asked the girl, who had still made no move to leave the water.

"I just keep thinking of a few more things I need to know," Marcie replied. Grey didn't look at her.

He took Judith's arm and turned her back toward the house. "Why don't we get something to drink for all of us?"

"All right." Judith gave their guest one more smile and looked quizzically at Grey as they walked toward the house.

Grey glanced back once before they reached the door. Marcie had finally climbed out of the pool. In one hand she held her discarded blouse and with the other she was reaching behind her back to unhook to top of her bikini. When she saw Grey looking at her she gave him a little smile as if the two of them shared a secret. Grey hastily turned away and opened the back door of the house for Judith. She looked at him curiously again. "You certainly are jumpy today."

"Spring fever," he said, and felt immediately that was the wrong thing to have said.

# 5

EVEN WHILE HE WAS WORKING GREY VAGUELY kept track of what was going on in the house, so when he heard the knocking at the front door he knew that Judith was upstairs with Katy.

"I'll get it," he called, glad of the opportunity to take a break. He was starting a new chapter, on the judicial reforms of Henry II, and every opening sentence he wrote launched him on a slightly different course than the one he wanted. His mind was stuck. Words continued to rearrange themselves in his thoughts as he opened the front door and rubbed his eyes.

If the man on the doorstep had spoken, Grey would have been returned to the real world more quickly. As it was, it was a few seconds before he realized that he and his visitor were both standing there without speaking. But if Grey was adrift, Simon was intense. He stood staring at his former attorney, his eyes flat and opaque, looking like a carved statue left on Grey's doorsill.

"Can I—?" Grey began, then paused and looked more closely at Simon. "May I help you?" he finally finished.

Simon continued to stare at him. Grey thought about closing the door quietly in his face. What stopped him was a familiarity about the man, and Grey's conviction that the visitor would still be standing there silently the next time the door was opened.

"Don't know me?" Simon finally said. His voice was flat too.

Grey felt himself grow instantly weary. "Tell me who you are."

Simon let too long a pause go by again before speaking. "I think you got my money," he said quietly. "Kind of insultin' not to remember the name of a fella you robbed."

Grey could see a long discussion ensuing, which accounted for his weariness. Stubbornness was written all over the man in front of him. Grey tried to cut through the beginnings of the argument in hopes of settling it quickly.

"How much am I supposed to have taken?"

Simon smiled. His mouth didn't move, but his eyes took on some life. "Ya do know me then."

Grey sighed. "No. Just tell me."

"Simon Hocksley."

Grey started nodding as soon as the man opened his mouth. He had almost recognized him. "Right, right. Glad to see you out, Mr. Hocksley. Now, if you're referring to your bill, I'd have to look it up, but I believe—"

Simon spat into the gardenia bush beside the door. "Ya took my money. It was th' only money I had ta pay ya with. I told ya where it was hid so's you could take yer fee outta that. But you took the whole thing."

The explanation revived Grey's energy. "Come on. You mean to say you told me where the loot was hidden, after going to all the trouble of stealing it?"

Hands on hips, Simon nodded, leaving his eyes downcast. "I believe I did."

"No you don't. I'm sorry if the money's gone, Mr. Hocksley, but you're grasping at straws. You know you wouldn't have told me where it was. You must have told someone else. Did you have a partner?"

Simon ignored the question. "Ya followed me, then."

Grey just shook his head.

Simon looked around, casting his eyes up at an angle as if he could see through the walls and all the way through the house to the backyard. Grey had the sudden impression that Simon had spent time watching the house before coming to the door. Simon's next words confirmed it.

"Nice house. Nice pool in the back, too. Takes money."

"I make money. My wife works, too." The lie seemed to be called for. "How much money are we talking about?" Grey added after another pause.

Simon turned sly. "'F you already know, no need me tellin' ya. 'F you don't know, you ain't ever gonna know."

That triumph seemed to satisfy him for the moment. The two men stood looking at each other. The silence ended behind Grey's back, with footsteps on the stairs. Grey saw Simon look past him and then back into his face. His tiny smile returned.

"Pretty wife."

Knowing already that the stairs couldn't be seen from the front door, Grey turned and looked. The long hall behind him was empty and there was no sign of Judith in the narrow slice of living room that could be seen from the front door alcove. Grey stepped out onto the porch, pulling the door shut behind him. He continued to return Simon's stare. "I don't have your money," he said again.

"Maybe you don't." Simon no longer looked displeased. "But I'll tell you this." His smile was gone very suddenly. He raised a long fore-finger and held it firmly under Grey's chin. Grey kept his head down against the pressure, grimacing only slightly. "I aint goin' anywhere," Simon said. "And I'm gonna have my money back."

The fingernail pressing under Grey's chin was jagged and the gritty dirt under the nail was being embedded in his skin. He could imagine various nasty diseases crawling onto his face.

Simon seemed to know just when Grey was about to reach and knock the hand away. Abruptly he gave a small twist to his finger, dropped the hand, and turned away. He strode away quickly, not looking back. Grey stood watching him, fingering his chin where Simon's dirty fingernail had broken the skin and left a thin line of blood.

Grey had almost forgotten the incident by the next day, when he was back in Austin. He had dealt with threats before, though Simon's foul breath on his face and finger under his chin had given this one a very personal quality. The conventional wisdom was that people who made threats did not carry them out. Grey hoped for once the conventional wisdom would prove correct.

So he was untroubled as he walked slowly through the stacks in the University of Texas library again. Walls of books separated him from any problems the real world might have presented. But not for long.

Hands covered his eyes from behind his

back, and a low voice said, "What are you doing here?" For a terrifying instant it was as if the stacks had come alive, like the trees in Oz. Grey hastily freed himself and stepped forward, turning. When he recognized his assailant he said, with some annoyance in his voice, "Marcie."

She grinned at him. He didn't return the smile. "Hello," he said formally.

He was not happy to see her. She reminded him of the attraction to her he'd felt, and that stirred his sense of guilt. This free-floating, almost theoretical guilt was worse than if he'd actually done something, because this feeling could attach itself to even the most innocent behavior, such as talking to her in the library. He was also afraid he'd left her with the impression that the two of them shared an intimate secret.

"How did you ever find me?" she said. "Did one of my roommates tell you I was here?"

"I didn't find you," Grey said stiffly. "I'm in here doing some research of my own. And I don't really have enough time—"

"I thought you'd go to the law library for your kind of material," Marcie said with interest. She had taken a step forward to narrow the distance between them again. Grey refused to keep retreating from her. He did wish, though, that a librarian would come hurrying up to tell them to stop talking.

"Sometimes I do, but a lot of the books are here. I've got—"

"Anyway, I'm glad to see you," she said. "I was going to give you a call later. Do you think we could go somewhere and talk? It'll just take a minute, I swear."

"Say," Grey said suddenly, forgetting to be cold. "You talked to Simon Hocksley, didn't you?"

"What? Me?"

"Yes. You got him a little stirred up, you might like to know."

"But I haven't seen him yet."

"You haven't?" Grey said.

"No, what's he done? But wait, let's go somewhere we can talk. I've got some more things I need to ask you before I do talk to him."

"No, I don't think so."

Marcie looked at him closely for the first time and his expression dampened her mood. "I was afraid of this," she said. "That you'd start feeling guilty and then decide it was my fault and get mad at me—"

"I'm not mad," Grey said. "I just don't have—"

"But I really do need your help. It's too late to pick another topic now. If you're worried about being seen with me we could go someplace where no one would see you. We could go to my apartment, and take separate cars—"

"No, no," Grey said, wondering if she could

possibly mean the invitation to be innocent. "I just don't have the time today."

"Oh. All right." She brightened again. "Well, I could come to your house again. It's no trouble. When would be convenient for you?"

Never would be convenient for me, he thought. He wished she didn't know where he lived. He sighed and looked at his watch.

"All right," he said. "We'll do it now. But this will be the last time, right?"

"Whatever you say." She grinned broadly. When she'd been unsure of herself a moment earlier she'd had a little-girl look, but her smile wiped away every trace of that. It was the same knowing look she'd displayed at his pool, as if Grey had again put himself in her debt. He didn't like her smile. It seemed to say that he was conceding much more than one more interview.

# 6

JUDITH STARTED DOWN THE STAIRS, GOT HALF-way, sensed the presence behind her, and turned around. Katy stood at the top of the stairs, swaying.

"Katy!" Judith clapped her hands to draw the baby's attention. Katy was staring at the stairs themselves, hypnotized. She looked up at her mother at the noise of the handclap.

"Turn around," Judith said. "You want to come down? Turn around." She moved one finger in a circle. They were trying to teach Katy to come down the stairs backwards, using her hands. She always wanted to walk like an adult, but her legs weren't long enough.

Judith took two steps upward, hoping the movement wouldn't induce Katy to come to her. The stairs were uncarpeted, hard-edged, lethal. Grey had installed a baby gate at the top of the stairs but Judith hadn't pulled it closed because it usually creaked, and she'd been afraid of waking the baby she had just left in bed. This was the first time Katy had been able to climb out of her crib by herself, too.

"Turn around," Judith said again. "Katy! Turn around." If someone lifted the baby and turned her around, she would obediently come down the stairs that way, safely. But as long as she was facing Judith she wouldn't turn away from her. She couldn't interpret the hand signals or the words.

Katy lifted one foot and Judith started up the stairs. Katy reached downward for the next step and came nowhere near it. Her mouth opened in frustration; she swayed harder for a moment and abruptly sat down hard on the top step.

Judith reached her then, and swooped her up before she could start crying. Judith held her very tightly, thinking terrible thoughts about herself. It would have been entirely her fault if the baby had fallen down the stairs, and it would have been just as dangerous as a fall from the roof. She suddenly realized that this was just how Grey had been feeling. She had understood that he felt guilty and sorry, but understanding was not the same as experiencing the same feelings herself.

Katy's eyes were wide and blinking. Judith laughed and raised the baby high, softening the sting of the lesson Katy had just learned. She should have let her start crying, teach her to stay away from those stairs, but the pain on Katy's face was too immediate. "It's all right," Judith soothed. "It's all right. Just don't do it again." Katy wasn't capable of understanding these mixed signals. She smiled happily. I know what I'm doing, Judith thought: teaching her that following me down the stairs is fun. Well, she'd learn soon enough.

"Why aren't you asleep?" she chided. "What do you want? What does the baby want?"

She had thought Katy was asleep when she'd left her in the nursery. Katy had been, almost, but she couldn't stand the idea of missing something. Judith laughed at her as she yawned, and carried her downstairs. As she passed a living room window Judith glimpsed a man outside, across the road. She had only an impression of thinness, dirt, and a black slouch hat as she hurried past.

From the kitchen she retrieved Katy's bottle. The milk was still warm, and there was enough left to put her to sleep for real this time. Judith returned to the living room and sat on the sofa to feed the baby. Katy took the bottle readily, her eyes rolling and one hand moving rhythmically.

Judith looked out the window. The man was still there, forty yards away, in no hurry to leave. Pedestrians were so rare in this area that Judith watched him as curiously as if he'd been performing magic tricks. He would have drawn her attention anyway because she had never seen anyone like him: ragged, skinny, his face halfway between bearded and just needing a shave. There was a dog with him, a long brown mongrel with floppy ears, its nose to the ground. The man ignored the dog, instead looking in the general direction of the house, but not at Judith. He was so foreign to her that she stared at him through the picture window as impersonally as she would have watched a TV screen. When they had first moved to the country Judith had joked to Grey that their neighbors would be hillbillies, but now that she saw one, he wasn't funny.

The man's head turned and his gaze swept across Judith, startling her out of illusion. The window was no TV screen; it was large and clean and revealed her as clearly as it did him.

The movement of Katy's hand stopped. Judith looked down to see that the bottle was empty. She removed it gently and dabbed at Katy's mouth. The baby didn't open her eyes. Her mouth stayed open after Judith had wiped it clean. Everyone will smile at a sleeping baby. Judith did so, then stood up as quietly as she could. The view through the window forgotten, she started up the stairs, shifting Katy to her shoulder.

This time she stayed with her until she was certain she was asleep in the nursery bed.

Judith did some quiet straightening in the room and arranged the bedclothes. Five minutes passed.

Judith heard the faintest of clicks from downstairs, then what sounded like a light footfall. She frowned and looked at the baby. She hadn't heard a car. She stepped to the doorway and softly called, "Grey?"

There was no answer except from Katy. Katy's eyelids fluttered for an instant, her mouth snapped closed. Judith stepped to her side, quietly saying, "Shhh. Shhhh. Sleep, baby. Sleep."

Reassured on some subliminal level, the baby fell restfully asleep again. Judith stayed with her for a few minutes to be sure, then backed quietly out of the nursery. She stood in the hallway listening for a moment, then started down the stairs.

It came as a sudden revelation to Grey that he was not enjoying himself. That was a happy thought. He hadn't wanted to come to the coffee shop with Marcie, he only had because of her intention to keep bothering him at home otherwise. So in a way he was here in defense of his home; but if he'd been enjoying himself, that reasoning wouldn't have stood up.

Marcie was doing her best. She was very animated today, and every time he thought he had a chance to bring the conversation to a conclusion she thought of one more question. Finally he said, "Wouldn't Simon Hocksley be able to tell you some of this better than I can?"

"Well—" She hesitated for a long time, not meeting his eyes. "I'm not sure anymore that I will talk to him. You can tell I've been putting it off, can't you? To tell you the truth, he still scares me to death. I feel funny about . . . You know, it was a woman he attacked before."

"That was a different situation. I'm sure you wouldn't have anything to worry about, as long as you don't have anything he wants."

"Well thanks," she said, mock-huffily.

"You know what I mean." Grey smiled very mildly. "I've got to be getting home. That was all you wanted, wasn't it?" he added with a certain firmness to his tone.

"Oh yes, thank you." Marcie stood up hastily herself. "Listen, I really appreciate your help. I couldn't have—"

Grey was thinking of his home and hoping she wouldn't bother him again. Clichés suddenly clogged his throat: We've got to stop meeting like this. I love my wife. The child to think of.

"This should about wrap it up for us, shouldn't it?" he said.

"Yes." Marcie finally looked slightly abashed. "If I . . . No, I'm sure that will do it. Thanks a lot again. I'll send you a copy of the paper."

Leaving the coffee shop, Grey glanced at his

watch. He felt unreasonably guilty about the time just spent with Marcie, almost as if he'd been having an affair. He was suddenly anxious to get home. Once outside he hurried down the sidewalk, fleetingly thinking of himself as a blurred image in a private detective's camera.

He couldn't stop acting furtive. On the drive home he tried to think of an excuse for having been gone this long, where no excuse was needed. Judith never interrogated him. The drive calmed him. At least this time he had nothing on his breath but coffee and cheese Danish.

He came through the back door softly, as if he could slip in and insinuate himself slyly into his family, so craftily that they wouldn't even realize he had been gone. Realizing the ridiculousness of creeping into the house in broad daylight, he closed the door behind him even more forcefully than usual. His heels clicked on the linoleum as he crossed the empty kitchen, calling Judith's name.

There was no answer from her. He turned right, down the short hallway to the living room, which was also as empty of company as the view outside. "Judith?" he called again, more quietly.

Slightly worried, he dropped his jacket on the sofa and started back toward the stairs. He was on the first one when her legs came into view above him. She opened the baby gate and came down, carrying Katy. The baby reached for Grey and Judith handed her over, but almost immediately Katy wanted down. As soon as he put her on her feet Judith stepped in close, put her arms around his neck, and kissed him.

"What's wrong?" he asked.

"Nothing, I'm just glad to see you."

"Oh, that."

They kissed again, holding each other. It was the most warmth Judith had shown him since she'd seen Katy on the roof, and Grey realized how much he had missed it. He felt at home again. In the back of his mind he knew there must be some reason for it, but he didn't ask what it was and Judith didn't volunteer anything about the adventure of the unlocked baby gate. One of the nice things about their marriage was that they could let questions go sometimes. After four years they still had small secrets from each other, they hadn't blended into one person.

They sat on the sofa for a while, watching dusk gradually destroy the fine tuning of the view outside. In half an hour they were in darkness. Judith snapped on a lamp and blinked.

"Like a drink?" Grey asked. She nodded a little sleepily.

"Anything fascinating happen today?" he

called from the kitchen as he clunked ice cubes into glasses. Judith shook her head. "Not a thing," she amplified when he returned.

Grey moved his books to make room for the glasses on the coffee table. "Let me just put these in the study."

When he came back he was frowning slightly. "Did Katy go in the study?"

"No. I kept the door closed."

Grey sat, but was still preoccupied. "Did *you* go in?" Judith shook her head.

Still frowning, Grey stood up and walked slowly back into the study. Judith followed him, unconcerned.

"I didn't leave it like this," Grey said.

Judith shrugged. The room was a little messy, but nothing very out of the ordinary. "Maybe she's learning to open doors," she said lightly.

Grey sat behind his disordered desk and speculatively opened a couple of drawers. "Nothing missing, I guess." He looked at Judith, who shrugged again and went back to her drink.

"What have you gotten yourself into, Grey?"

It was Harry's continuing conceit that he never got invited to Grey's house. He had been there half a dozen times in the year and few months they'd lived here, but every time he came he pretended it was his premier visit.

Harry stood on the front porch now with his

arms extended, showing off the green hills and the empty road as if they were his own exhibits. "All this peace and solitude out here, somebody'd have to come tell you if the world ended. How can you stand it?"

Fran, standing impatiently behind Harry, finally knocked one of his arms down and brushed past him. She hugged Grey quickly, transferred it to Judith, and went on into the house. "Let me away from him, I've already heard this one. Were you intendin' to offer me a drink, honey?"

Judith followed Fran's jovial voice into the house, while Grey stayed in the doorway, smiling through Harry's harangue.

"This is just no place for a person, Grey. You're going to turn bucolic on me." Harry shook his head and let himself be led inside.

"You want a place just like it, don't you, Harry?"

"Hell, I got *away* from the country."

They entered the living room to see Fran on the sofa, supporting Katy on her lap with one hand and casually keeping her drink out of the baby's reach with the other. "Who's the prettiest baby? Who is? Can you say Aunt Fran? Sure. Aunt Frances? She's going to be a drinker, Grey. Let me know when she's ready and I'll come out and teach her how to pass out like a lady."

Judith was standing close at hand, smiling

politely. When Grey came into the room she tacitly left the baby in his care and returned to the kitchen for her own drink.

"What'll you have, Harry?" she called.

"Oh, let me think for a minute." It was a ritual. Judith knew Harry's invariable drink was bourbon.

Fran had managed to transfer Katy's attention from her glass to her finger, which Katy gripped with both hands, so tightly Fran could swing her gently from side to side, her smile matching the baby's. "Isn't she the darlingest thing, Harry?" she said without taking her eyes from the baby's.

"Yeah," Harry grunted.

"You have all the feelings of a cow flop in winter," she told him. Then to Katy, sweetly: "Doesn't he? That's right. Uncle Harry's just a nasty old shithead, isn't he? Yes."

Judith returned gripping three glasses. Harry took the brown one. Grey and Judith had the wineglasses. After one sip and a nod of thanks, Harry said, "Well, let's see this damned masterpiece that's keeping you rusticating out here."

"We're a terrible influence on the baby, aren't we?" Fran said to Judith.

"She knows better than to pay any attention to us," Harry said, standing. "Come on, Grey."

"We try to expose her to all kinds," Judith said lightly.

"It's not ready to be shown around yet," Grey demurred.

"That's what we are, all kinds," Fran said happily. "I just want to read the sexy parts, Grey. Why don't you underline 'em for me?"

Harry hauled Grey up out of his chair and started him toward the study, over his continuing protests. Harry shut the study door behind them and Grey pushed the manuscript toward him. Harry only glanced at a couple of sentences and immediately lost the interest he'd feigned. "You're not ready to give it up yet?"

Grey shook his head indulgently. "A little more time, Harry."

Harry was nodding, looking around the room, his question already forgotten. "I guess you're really writing it," he finally said. "I thought you might have a rubber girl hidden in here or something."

He shifted his feet, looking all around the small room. Grey watched him, waiting for the more Harry obviously had to say. Harry met his eyes, ducked away, and reluctantly came out with it.

"That, uh, that girl you sent around to the office—"

"What girl?"

"You know, she had some questions, name was—"

"Marcie."

"Yeah, Marcie."

Grey understood now Harry's reluctance to bring up the subject. "Yeah, that was a great job, Harry. You must have given her a terrific idea of legal ethics, practically jumping on her when she came in—"

"Jumping? Hell, I didn't close the door while she was in my office. I wouldn't do that, Grey, your girl—"

"My girl? Christ, Harry, I don't have a girl. Certainly not—"

"She told me, Grey, she said you were 'good friends.' Like that: you know, *good friends*."

Grey kept his voice down. "Harry, I don't care what she told you—" At the same time he was wondering just what Marcie had said to his partner. Even without lying, just by coloring events slightly—say, their time in the pool together—Marcie could have made Grey sound bad.

The men weren't looking at each other. Harry looked as embarrassed as Grey. He watched his own fingers play on the desktop. "Hey, it's none of my business anyway."

"Believe me, there's nothing going on," Grey said, sounding insincere even to himself.

"Good. Fran will be glad to hear it." To Grey's surprised look he added, "Fran didn't like her looks. You can imagine. She's the one who wanted me to talk to you."

"Oh yeah?" Grey said. "You were going to set me straight?"

"Something spooky about that girl," Harry said curiously. "She reminded me of those women who write to prison inmates, you know?" He saw that his glass was empty and said in a stronger voice, "Well, I'm glad we could have this little chat. Let's get the hell out of here."

Later, after dinner, Harry and Grey went upstairs for a game of pool in the game room. Judith and Fran followed, keeping one eye on the game and carrying on their own desultory conversation.

Harry's game was to slam the balls around at least four cushions and break up clusters of balls to little purpose. It always looked like an accident when a ball went in, but after every shot Harry nodded judiciously, as if his unknown plan were proceeding perfectly. Grey took his time looking for the best shots and precisely dropping them in. To obscure the fact that he was trouncing his guest he asked, "So how are things in the office?"

Fran broke off what she was telling Judith to say emphatically, "It's just like the state penitentiary except without their high standards."

Grey, dropping in a ball and moving around the table to another, said, "Any of my old clients ever come in and ask after me?"

"Nah," Harry said. "You know, those prison escapees try to keep a low profile."

"Somebody did come by just yesterday," Fran said. "I was meaning to tell you about him. Talk about scary. Old caved-in black hat, muddy boots. Needed a shave bad and a bath worse. Smelled so various, you know, I could not only smell him, I could tell what *parts* of him I was smellin'. I kept my eye on him every second."

Harry said, "I figured he was one of Fran's kin, and I stayed clear of him."

Neither Grey nor Judith laughed. Both of them were frowning slightly. "What was his name?" Grey asked.

"Wouldn't tell me."

"Then tell me a little more about what he looked like."

After a few seconds' description Grey started nodding. "Simon Hocksley, I'll bet. What did he want?"

"I don't know, but whatever it was, he wanted it bad. Just said he had to see you, nobody else would do. I told him you wouldn't be in, but he didn't believe me. He finally left, but when I left for the day he was in the parking lot, hanging around my car. I didn't like that a bit, let me tell you. I finally told him you'd been appointed a special adviser to the President and you wouldn't be back at the office. I don't think he believed the first part."

Grey winced. "I wish you hadn't told him I'd quit working."

"Why?"

"He'll think I must've come into some money suddenly to retire like that."

"Who is he?" Harry asked. "You owe him money or something?"

Grey told them the little he knew. It was news to Judith, too. At the time it hadn't seemed worth telling her about the visit.

"I saw somebody like that," Judith said thoughtfully.

"When?" Grey said sharply. Harry and Fran looked back and forth between the Stantons.

"Yesterday. Remember when you said you thought somebody had been in your study? I saw him outside, across the road with a dog. Then when I came up here with Katy I thought I heard someone come in. But when I came down there was no one there."

There was a short silence which came to center on Grey. The other three watched him seriously. "You think he's dangerous?" Fran asked.

Grey shrugged off the question. "He just wants his money."

"Don't mess with him," Harry said. "He's out on parole. Tell his parole officer he was trespassing and get him slapped back inside."

"Can't prove anything," Grey said. "Besides, I don't want to put him back in jail. He just got out."

"So what?" Harry said seriously. "You gotta protect your own ass."

Grey found himself wandering out onto the terrace, and the others followed. It could not be said that the night was impenetrable. Away from the city lights the sky was powdered with stars, an unpatched roof leaking plenty of light down on them. But the ground was dark enough, full of hiding places.

"I wouldn't worry about it," Judith said, standing in the lighted doorway with the baby in her arms. Harry and Fran looked skeptical.

"Yeah," Grey told them. "He probably won't even be back."

They went back inside to finish the game.

# 7

"It's too cold."

"She wants in."

"And she always will, if we let her in this time."

"Not if it really is too cold. If it is, she'll want right back out."

Grey was in the shallow end of the pool, one arm stretched up to hold Katy at bay. She pushed steadily against him, leaning forward and trying with both hands to remove the hand that kept her from the water. Grey shifted from hand to hand. Katy's small fingers scratched him and he was losing his footing. Judith sat on the pool apron a few feet away, ignoring the struggle.

"Help."

"Let her in if she wants," Judith said without looking at them. "We keep saying we're going to teach her."

"Dadadadadada," Katy said, a sign she was growing angry. She tugged fiercely at Grey's fingers.

"Come in and help," Grey said to Judith.

"I will in a minute." Her eyes were closed, her face lifted to the sun. She looked pale even in her white one-piece suit. Her blond hair was piled loosely on top of her head, trapping the light in its whorls. She looked like a creature materializing out of a sunbeam. The orange towel on which she sat was the only color that touched her.

Katy almost slipped over Grey's hand. "All right," he said. He stood a little higher and picked her up under both armpits. "You're not going to like it," he assured her, but she was already gurgling happily, stretching her feet toward the water.

Grey lowered her slowly. When her feet reached the cool water she instantly drew them up, squatting in midair where he held her. She gasped and her mouth turned into a comical O. Grey laughed and held her against his chest. Judith looked at them and smiled.

Katy still wanted the water. She reached for it, leaning out away from Grey. He held her horizontally above the water, low enough that she could reach it. She slapped at the water with both hands, splashing it in her own face. When she saw her parents laughing she attacked it even more enthusiastically, raising her voice in a joyful ululation.

"Let her down," Judith said. She had given up her contemplation of the sun to watch the two of them in the pool.

"All right," Grey said. To Katy: "Mommy says. Here we go. Are you ready? Ooooh."

Katy joined him in the last expression as he lowered her to the water. She kicked and slapped at the surface, holding her head away. Grey thought she was scared, but when he raised her away she reached for the water, whimpering. Grey lowered her and she was happy again.

"You said you were coming in," Grey said to Judith.

"I changed my mind." She smiled.

"No you didn't." Grey started walking toward Judith's side of the pool. Katy liked the movement. "Wooooo."

"That's right. Tell Mommy to come in. Say, 'It's fun, Mommy.'"

When they reached the side Grey raised Katy so that she saw her mother. She smiled, patted Judith's ankle, and with the other hand splashed the water.

"Come on. Help me teach her."

"Noooo . . ."

"Fun, Mommy," Katy said suddenly. Grey and Judith laughed uproariously but Katy couldn't see what the fuss was about and they couldn't get her to say it again. The baby looked at them as if there were no reason to repeat herself, especially since they said the phrase over and over themselves.

"Well, now you have to come in," Grey said.

"I don't want to get my hair wet."

"I wondered how long it would be before you'd use that one."

The lazy argument ended with Judith stepping gingerly into the pool. They held Katy between them and lowered her into the water, where she quickly developed what her father considered an inordinate fondness for putting her face underwater. After a while they put her on the air mattress between them and drifted around the pool. When he looked down Grey could see Judith's legs moving palely, looking jointless. She noticed him watching and became even more languid, closing her eyes. She looked thoughtful, but he couldn't guess what she was thinking. When she finally spoke it was:

"Do you think Harry and Fran are having an affair?"

Grey laughed. Judith looked at him for an explanation.

"You've heard how they talk to each other," he said.

"That's what I mean. Don't you think it sounds . . . intimate?"

"It's always sounded to me like they don't like each other much."

She considered that, but shook her head.

"Well," Grey concluded, "I've never caught them smooching in the office, so I don't think it's something we need to worry about."

"No one ever caught us in my office," Judith said. Her leg brushed his under the air mattress.

"But don't you think the secretaries used to wonder why we had to keep meeting for weeks after you'd turned down my loan application?"

"They could see I'd taken pity on you." Judith's eyes were still closed but she smiled when he did. When her leg brushed his again he caught it near the knee. Her smile broadened a bit when he shifted his hold to her thigh.

Katy broke that up by falling off into the water. Both of them swooped down on her, lifting her out an instant after she'd gone under. She didn't have time to be scared until they were holding her up and wiping her face. They tried to soothe her with kisses and laughter and demonstrations in which they, one at a time, put their faces underwater too. Katy decided she liked it. They let her back into the water when she badgered them into it, but this time they held her floating on her stomach, and tried to get her to kick her feet. She wouldn't understand their object for long minutes. Then she would suddenly kick wildly for a few seconds, but when they laughed and approved she stopped, not knowing what she'd done. She was having fun, though, and they kept at it.

Judith was the first to look up. She gasped, the intake of breath frightening because it was so quick and low. Grey turned, gripping Katy's arm too tightly, so that the baby looked up as well, and for a moment they offered a family portrait in fright.

Simon Hocksley stood above them, wearing a thin smile. He wore the same black hat and held a rifle loosely in one hand. "Howdy," he said. His unbelievable smile didn't make his face more pleasant.

No one answered him until Judith put a hand on Grey's arm and hesitantly offered, "Hello."

"Nice ta see you folks enjoying yourselves." He looked up at the sun, gauging its strength. "Haven't had a swim yet this year myself. Not in three years, in fact."

Grey, after making sure Judith had the baby, edged away from his family. Judith's hand was reluctant to let him go. His own hand moved underwater, urging them toward the opposite side of the pool. He couldn't tell if Judith had seen the movement or not.

Simon, without looking down, took a slow step along the side of the pool, then another, following Grey's progress. When he looked down they were still parallel, Simon's head five feet above Grey's.

"What brings you here?" Grey asked. He was rising higher in the shallow end of the pool, high enough to see that there was no one else around, not even the dog. There was also nothing that looked like a weapon, except in Simon's hand. The pool area suddenly looked very bare to Grey: an orange towel, two ragged lawn chairs, the inflated raft. He was glad to see that Judith had moved back as he'd directed, but she was still in the pool, in deeper water. Katy clung to her, looking at Simon and then at her parents.

"Jest out fer a stroll," Simon said. "Haven't gotten used ta bein' out yet. It's real nice, ya know?"

"I imagine," Grey said. His voice was flat, inoffensive, uninviting. He was still moving into shallower water, and Simon was still following him along the edge of the pool. Simon turned the corner and stood at the spot Grey had been heading for. Grey stopped in the water. After a pause he said, "You know you're violating your parole by trespassing?"

"I'm sorry about that," Simon said. His face slid easily into an expression of apology. "I'as just comin' cross-country and I didn't really realize where I'as at."

Grey started moving toward another exit spot, stopped when Simon shadowed his movement. "Carrying the gun's a violation too."

Simon held up the small rifle and looked at it carelessly. "Squirrel gun," he said deprecatingly. "I don't think they'd begrudge it, d'you? They wouldn't want ta let me out 'n then have me starve ta death, would they?"

"They wouldn't want to take you back, either, but they will if you violate the terms of your parole." Grey realized the ridiculousness of his stern tone, but no other tone would have been appropriate either. He wished he were dressed and standing on Simon's level. Somehow a shirt would have made him less vulnerable to attack.

Simon suddenly squatted at the edge of the pool and thrust his face forward. The movement was threatening, but his voice remained mild. "But you won't tell 'em, will ya? You wouldn't wanta do that ta me."

They stared at each other until Simon seemed to feel he'd received an answer. "Guess what I found out?" he asked. He leaned back and looked farther down the pool. Grey glanced back there. Judith and Katy were still in the water, Judith clinging to the ladder in the deep end. Simon stared at her, his eyes moving.

"What?" Grey said, drawing Simon's attention back to himself.

It took Simon a moment to gather his thoughts. He smiled again. "I found out you lied to me. You quit your job. And any fool can see that yer lovely wife there has better things to do than work for a living. Y'all jest seem ta be independently wealthy."

"We've been saving for years."

Simon laughed shortly. "Me too."

When Simon's stare returned to Judith, Grey felt something drain out of him: the fear, maybe, or his good sense. He felt empty and cold. He finally began walking toward Simon, moving against the drag of the water. Judith said his name.

Grey planted his palms on the apron and levered himself up. When he got one foot up, his balance was very delicate, but Simon didn't move to push him back in. Grey stood up in front of the intruder.

"I haven't got your money," he said in a low voice. "I told you that once. If you come around here again—"

Simon cut him off. "You've got the money all right." His voice was still low, but immovable. "Yesterday I got a tracking bloodhound, and he led me from where I buried it to right here."

Judith started saying something but they both ignored her.

"I know you've got it," Simon said. "Don't worry about that. And don't worry about me gettin' it back, either. I surely will." He grinned coldly. "Remember how I got it in the first place."

They stood together. The rifle stretched between them, from Simon's hand to a point near Grey's knee. They stood there until Grey began to wonder what would ever move them. Then Simon looked aside, down into the pool. He raised one finger to the brim of his hat, smiled slightly, and turned away. He moved slowly, past the house, across the road, toward trees in the distance. His figure remained a part of the landscape for a long time.

Grey heard water breaking as Judith came up the ladder. She came to stand beside him.

"Grey?"

He watched the shambling figure move toward the trees.

"What are you going to do?"

Grey was moving one finger back and forth along the underside of his chin.

That was the afternoon. In the evening, Marcie came.

Grey and Judith looked at each other apprehensively when the bell rang. They sat close on the sofa with the curtains drawn. Katy was between them. Neither of them moved. The bell rang again. Katy tried to climb off the sofa as if she would answer it herself.

That was decisive. If Grey had been alone he would have sat there until the menace at the door went away. As it was, he walked slowly out of the room and turned right into the alcove at the front door.

For an instant it was a relief to see Marcie through the peephole. Anything was preferable to the man with the gun he'd expected. Relief was quickly replaced by irritation, however. The first time or two Grey had been flattered by her reliance on his help and even by her flirting. It had been a while since anyone except his wife had flirted with him. But Marcie was quickly becoming something more than a nuisance. She stood there already in character, face smooth, smiling slightly, eyes focused on nothing in particular, as if she were practicing innocent expressions. She wore a dress and dangled a small handbag in front of her. She looked like a teenager traveling alone for the first time, waiting to meet her uncle on a train platform.

When she raised her fist again Grey opened the door quickly, almost pulling it into his nose. Marcie was left standing off-balance, one hand raised to knock on nothing. She smiled at the awkwardness of her stance but Grey didn't return it. "Hello," he said levelly, not moving out of the doorway.

"Hello, Mr. Stanton. I'm back for one final interview. Hope you don't mind. Just one or two things I want to get perfectly straight before I interview Mr. Hocksley."

Her voice was louder than necessary. She stood there confident of being invited inside.

"I thought we had already answered all your questions."

"I thought so too, Mr. Stanton, until I started putting together the questions to ask Mr. Hocksley, and I realized . . . I *am* sorry this is turning out more complicated than I expected, but it's just too late for me to pick another topic now. I promise—"

"Grey? Who is it?"

Grey still hadn't moved, but when he turned to call over his shoulder, Marcie slipped past him and into the living room. "It's only me, Mrs. Stanton," she said brightly.

Judith stood with her hand on the telephone. She remained frozen for a moment when the near-stranger entered her living room, but she made the transition more quickly than Grey had.

"Hello. Miss Willis, isn't it?"

"Marcie."

The two women smiled at each other. Judith's smile was a multileveled artifact that made Marcie's look childish.

"What brings you to see us this time?" Judith asked graciously.

"I just wanted to ask your husband a few more questions. I promise this will be the last time."

"Nonsense. We love having you."

Grey chose that moment to enter the living

room. Marcie hadn't wilted under Judith's charm. Both of them turned smiles on him. He slouched in the doorway, looking sullen by comparison.

"I'll get us something to drink," Judith said. "Would you like coffee?"

When Judith left, Grey moved into the room. He sat on the sofa and looked at Marcie without invitation. It seemed to him that her smile became a bit conspiratorial. He ignored it.

When the three of them sat a few minutes later with their coffee cups, Marcie still didn't speak. She sat on an armchair facing the sofa, which was once again occupied by Grey and Judith. Marcie sat forward on the edge of her chair, apparently eager to be questioned. Judith looked curiously from her to Grey. He felt the glance and grudgingly acted the host.

"Well, what can we do for you?"

Instantly Marcie dug her notebook from her handbag and introduced a more serious expression. "Let me see. Oh. One thing. Who paid the fee when you defended Mr. Hocksley? Did he, or . . . ?"

She had two or three more questions like that, things they had already covered. After a few minutes of it Grey sat forward and interrupted her.

"What did Mr. Hocksley say about all this?"

"I haven't talked to him yet." Marcie sat with pen poised.

Grey and Judith looked at each other. "Someone has," Judith said to him.

"What's happened?" Marcie asked.

Grey paused before telling her. "Simon Hocksley's been around to see us."

"Really?" Marcie said seriously. "Well, I told you he'd just gotten out. Did he . . . he didn't blame you for his going to prison, did he?"

They told her the story of Simon's visit that afternoon. Marcie's look of concern grew stronger. Judith gave the bulk of the narrative.

"You must have been terrified," Marcie said.

"We did feel pretty helpless."

"Have you told the police?"

Judith gave Grey another concerned look as she said, "No."

Marcie nodded judiciously. "Probably just as well. You'd just come off looking silly, complaining just because a man cut across your yard while he was out walking. And all this is because he thinks you took his money?"

The last question was directed at Grey, so he nodded. He still hadn't given Marcie a hint of a friendly expression.

Marcie smiled again. "Did you? Take the money? No, I'm kidding, don't answer." Grey hadn't even considered answering.

Marcie turned to Judith. "I had thought of asking you a few questions too. I was wondering if just this kind of situation ever came up. Your husband sort of bringing his work home with him. But I can see it does. You must be used to it by now."

"No," Judith said. "No, this is my first experience with this sort of thing. You think we can expect it to keep happening?" she asked Grey only half-facetiously.

"I'm sure it won't come up again." Grey had moved closer to her on the sofa, and now he put his arm behind her so that they presented a small family group to Marcie. "Was there anything else?" he asked.

Marcie looked back and forth between them and finally shrugged. "Seems like there was something else, but I can't think what. Oh well, I guess it'll come to me."

When she rose to leave, Judith stayed seated, holding Katy. Grey saw Marcie to the front door and opened it immediately. She lingered, standing close to him.

"I'll let you know how my interview with Mr. Hocksley turns out," she said.

"That's all right, don't go to any trouble."

"But he might tell me something you'd need to know," she suggested.

"I strongly doubt that."

"You never can tell."

She seemed ready to say more, but Grey said, "Good night, Marcie," and after a hesitation she passed at her own unhurried pace into the night. Grey stood there with a thoughtful expression until he heard her car start. Judith's voice made him jump.

"Persistent girl, isn't she?"

Marcie dropped her purse into the passenger seat of her aged Datsun and took off. She smiled faintly to herself, and wouldn't have been able to tell an observer if the smile was real or just a holdover from the pleasant act she'd been putting on. Still, her mood was good. She was seldom dissatisfied for long. Life held too many possibilities, if you were clever enough to see them all.

In a few minutes she turned off the road onto a rutted dirt track. Night was deeper in the woods. The claws of the trees held the darkness in place so tightly that tatters of it would remain under the trees even after day came again. Marcie drove on with a reckless disregard for her car's undercarriage.

Waylon met her at the door. "Hi, sweetie," she greeted him, drumming her fingernails lightly on his stomach. She sauntered past him, hanging her purse on the antlers by the door. "What's going on?"

Waylon walked past her, keeping a wary eye on her, and sat in the wheelchair again. "He's not here," he said.

"Okay, I can wait." Marcie walked jauntily around the cluttered room, her heels loud on the wooden floor. The room smelled musty. All its surfaces were dusty: the sagging sofa and armchairs, the broken footstool, the ancient coffee table that teetered precariously on its three longest legs.

Waylon's hands were clasped in front of his mouth. He watched her over them. "What're you so happy about?"

"I'm always happy." She turned as if she were talking to a standing man, then exaggeratedly lowered her eyes. She put her hands on her hips and studied him. Waylon let her, saying nothing. "What is the big attraction of that thing, anyway?" she finally said.

Waylon shrugged, indicated the room with a sweep of his eyes. "Best piece of furniture in the house."

"But what made you get it in the first place?"

"Stole it from a junkyard for Daddy. That last year or so before he died—"

"Oh," Marcie said.

Waylon became more voluble for a minute. "But hey, no sense throwin' away a good chair, is there, just because nobody needs it?"

Marcie slowly crossed the room and moved behind him. Waylon lowered his hands to the armrests. Marcie put her hands on the handles behind the chair. "It's dumb, though," she said confidentially. Waylon looked up over his shoulder at her. "You keep using this thing and your legs are really going to waste away."

"Shit," Waylon said. He stretched the legs out in front of him. "I ain't worried."

"Then give me a ride," Marcie said. She sat in his lap and put her feet on the rests inside his. "Come on," she said impatiently, trying to move them. Waylon put his hands on the wheels and pushed.

"Wheee," Marcie said. She put an arm around his neck, and Waylon circled the room, rebounding from the broken furniture. He finally laughed with his passenger.

They were still at it ten minutes later when Simon came in. He grunted at the sight as he stopped to lean his rifle against the wall. "Knock that shit off," he said shortly.

Marcie jumped up from Waylon's lap. "Aw, he's grumpy. What's the matter, sweetie?"

Waylon had stopped the chair abruptly when Simon entered. Now he sat watching his immobile brother. Marcie was the only animated thing in the room. She put a hand on Simon's arm and led him further into the room. Waylon rolled back a few feet. "What's the matter?" Marcie asked again, wheedling.

"What were you doin' at that lawyer's house?" Simon asked.

Marcie grimaced across the room at Waylon and spoke as she would of a child. "He's jealous." She continued to Simon: "Sweetie, I just went there to ask about the money. And to see how they took your little talk this afternoon."

"What'd he say?" Simon was still standing stiffly.

"He *said* he didn't have it. What would you expect? But you've sure got 'em scared, honey." Marcie squeezed his upper arm more tightly. Simon nodded.

"He call the police?"

"No." Marcie glanced at Waylon, who watched the little scene from his corner vantage point.

Simon finally smiled. "Good," he said tightly. He looked down at the girl beside him, acknowledging her presence for the first time. He looked around the room, and his eyes barely caught on Waylon. "Come on," he said to Marcie. His arm went down across her back and the fingers of that hand splayed across her hip. She giggled as they crossed the room in step, Simon's arm holding her tightly against his side. They went through the door into the next room and Simon kicked it closed. Waylon sat in his wheelchair and stared at the closed door.

# 8

There was Simon, walking down the road. A blot on the bright afternoon. Judith saw him through the front window. He walked slowly, raising dust, his head down and his hands in his pockets. No urgency pushed him. Judith stood with her arms folded, studying him. Simon was as transparent as the window through which she watched him. He was clearly keeping an eye on them, but he wouldn't look up. He might have been passing an empty field. Judith was sure he saw her, but when he raised his head he elaborately looked in the opposite direction. Judith withdrew a step from the window. It was obvious Simon was going nowhere on the road, because half an hour later he was back, shuffling into sight from the opposite direction, and half an hour wasn't long enough to go anywhere and back on that road. Simon was guarding their house like a very slow sentry. In this broad daylight he looked thin and bent, not much of a menace.

A day or two later, the next time they saw him, he was back with the dog.

"See that? Grey? Come look at this."

Grey came in slowly from the study and stood beside his wife at the living room window.

"See? Remember my telling you how he acted the first time? Look at that. That dog never led him here."

The dog was snuffling along behind Simon, nose close to the ground, going off on tangents when it came across an interesting smell. It was clear the man had led the dog to the house and not the other way around.

"The dog's got more sense than he does," Judith said.

Grey grunted agreement.

"What does he think he's doing, amassing evidence?" she added.

Grey returned to his study, but Judith kept watching. At the far edge of the road Simon halted the dog, then looked carefully back and forth along the length of the road, an elaborate pantomime that assumed an audience. Judith obliged him by continuing to watch. After a few minutes Simon grew bored. He let the dog wander at will, only keeping him in the general vicinity of the Stanton house. The two of them were out there all afternoon, but Judith finally had better things to do.

They continued to see Simon, irregularly at first, then every day. A morning might pass without him, but he'd show up before sundown. Sometimes he was on duty the first time they looked out in the morning. He wasn't always visible in front of the house. Sometimes he was cutting across a field far behind it, a tiny figure outlined against the hills. That was the only time he looked up. Judith had the irrational feeling that he could see her clearly even when she could barely make him out. She stopped standing framed in the windows.

Sometimes Simon had the dog with him, sometimes he was alone. Occasionally he carried the rifle. Those were the times when he remained far from the house. But Judith, and Grey when he was watching, could see Simon swing the rifle up to his shoulder and sweep it around—sometimes, apparently, bringing it to bear on the house. A glint would catch her eye. Surely he didn't have a scope on a gun that small. Maybe he was carrying a different rifle now. Or maybe he wore binoculars when he was that far from the house.

The rifle wasn't just for show, whatever its effect on them. Judith watched once as Simon raised his gun in the distance and the dog went running after whatever he'd brought down. She forgot about it until several minutes later, when Simon passed close to the house while she was in the kitchen. Simon had a gun casually crooked through his elbow, and the dog waddled happily beside him. As Simon walked he plucked the bird he'd shot. The bird—Judith couldn't identify it—was already half-denuded, but it still seemed to flinch painfully every time Simon plucked another feather. Its wings were fallen open helplessly. Simon, crossing just beyond the pool, looked absorbed in his work. Judith watched with a frown of distaste. His fingers were dark and sticky; a few feathers clung to the backs of his hands.

Soon Simon's presence became a constant. It took on the character of a game: Find Simon in this picture. They knew every morning that he was there somewhere, even if they didn't see him. The day seemed unofficial until they'd had their first glimpse of him, the way some disease victims don't feel fully awake until the familiar pain returns.

One day, a week or so after it had started, Judith came downstairs in the afternoon to find Grey standing in the living room glaring out the window. Simon sat there across the road, unarmed today, his head moving back and forth as if he were watching a steady stream of traffic. The house still appeared to be invisible to him.

"Is he doing anything special?" Judith asked. She no longer bothered to keep close track of the daily show.

Grey shook his head. Judith stood with him for a minute. The ragged figure across the road paid them no attention. Grey sighed exasperatedly and turned on his heel.

"Where are you going?"

"Be back in a minute."

Grey's resolution dwindled after he was out the door, but he kept marching across the yard. The day was very warm, the sun lodged on the back of his neck. Grey kept his head down and his hands in his pockets, leaning forward against an unseen force. He raised a wall of dust when he crossed the road.

Simon was looking past Grey, away from the house. He didn't look up when Grey stood directly in front of him. The man could almost make you think you didn't exist.

"What the hell do you think you're doing?"

Simon slowly brought his gaze to bear on Grey. It climbed Grey's body like a physical thing, a small animal with sure claws. When the man's eyes met Grey's, Grey realized how shallow his own belligerence was in comparison; it was only a thin shield to hold between them.

"What do you think you're doing?" he repeated.

"Just sittin' here. Keepin' an eye on things."

"Why?"

Simon spat. "You know why."

Grey sighed, but kept his voice angry. "I don't have your money."

"You've got it," Simon said. Grey had become invisible again. Simon's eyes moved back and forth on the road.

"What makes you so sure?"

"You're th' only one could have it."

"You are just wrong. How can I change your mind?"

Simon said nothing. Grey stood with fists on hips, glaring down at him. Impasse again. Grey had the feeling there was a way to get through to the man, some magical phrase, if he could only think of it.

"I'm not going to put up with this," he finally said. Very lame statement. There wasn't much he could do about a man who chose to sit across the road from his house. Simon wasn't even trespassing anymore.

The words seemed to have had no impact on Simon, but after a pause he suddenly rose to his feet. Even without his rifle he was a couple of inches taller than Grey. His standing seemed to narrow the space between them. Grey involuntarily took a step back.

"You know how to put a stop to it," Simon

said quietly. When he said it he glowered at Grey. The next moment his eyes went opaque again. He looked over Grey's shoulder, then marched past him, brushing Grey's shoulder with his own.

Night. Blackness. Katy asleep one room away. The whole house shut down, a machine with the current dead. The blackness outside went uninterrupted within the house, so that the night was a solid block of obsidian: impenetrable, safe. Now they were really invisible.

Judith and Grey were in bed earlier than usual. They couldn't have said why. They hadn't been aware of what had made them uncomfortable as they sat in the living room, the only well-lighted cube of space for miles, but they had felt the relief when they'd turned off the last light and made the house just one more obscure piece of night.

Under the covers they felt added sanctuary. They kept the house very cool at night, using too much electricity, but it was worth it for the crisp air and the warmth of the bed. This far out from town it was reassuring to have something electrical running all night long. The hum of the air conditioner represented their lifeline to the outside world, still open.

A chuckle rose to Grey's throat. He couldn't suppress it. He felt like a kid at a slumber party.

"What is it?" Judith asked. She was a long

presence in the dark beside him, sharing his hiding place.

He turned and pulled her closer to him. She was wearing something very thin that gave off a faint aura of static electricity. Her arms and legs were bare. "I'm just happy," he said.

"Crazy." But her voice was very warm and happy too. She turned and put a hand on his stomach. He kissed her shoulder, the first part of her body his mouth found in the dark.

Theirs was the only warmth in the whole countryside. "I love you," they said simultaneously in low, darkness-smothered voices.

Judith laughed. "You're just saying that," she said. In the dark her voice was flirting, teasing, a separate entity for which she no longer felt responsible. Judith put her head back, elongating her neck, expanding the surface area of her skin. Grey was stroking her side and back, his hand curling and flattening.

The whisper of the air conditioner died as the thermostat shut off the automatic fan. They pushed the covers down around their waists. Grey reached inside her gown. His hands still moved very slowly. Judith was humming almost inaudibly; he felt the vibration of her throat. She rose to her knees, and Grey saw her outlined in the moonlight from the window as she pulled the gown off over her head.

"Don't think you're going to have your way with me," her playful voice said. She lay down full length against him. Their legs moved slowly, plaiting into a single strand of flesh as they kissed. Grey's hands explored down her body. Judith lay absolutely still for a moment, then suddenly laughed and pounced.

At some point the character of their lovemaking changed. It grew frantic, became flight rather than pursuit. Judith took charge, her teeth clenched, her throat constricted. A wave of previously unexpressed emotions seemed to grip her.

Grey was well aware of it. Sometimes his cool, knowing wife slipped free of her controls. It didn't happen often, but it seemed to happen most frequently during sex. As now, he would suddenly be aware of her great reserves of joy and strength and anger. At times like this her vitality made him worry for her. She was so full of life she seemed more vulnerable.

As soon as she collapsed onto his chest she clutched him tightly, her face turned down away from him. Grey held her strongly, his arms moving slightly, raising his head to kiss her hair. He knew from experience that there was no point in speaking. He reached down and pulled the covers over them, then gripped her again. They were as warm and safe as they could possibly be.

After long minutes he said, "Judith?"

She turned her head to face him. He could see her face dimly. She smiled.

"How are you?" he asked hesitantly.

Her smile broadened and she raised a hand to his face. Grey studied her expression. It was serene. He could very easily have been mistaken about her earlier reaction.

"What are you thinking about?"

Now it was Judith who laughed. "I'm wondering how many people would come if I threw a Tupperware party."

Grey smiled, but he was still serious. After looking at her searchingly, he said, "You're not worried about him, are you?"

She shook her head.

He cleared his throat and looked at the ceiling for a moment before looking back at her seriously and saying, "I want to tell you something. If anything ever happens to me—"

"Grey."

"No, I want to tell you. I don't mean with him. Necessarily. We should have talked about this before, anyway."

"Not now," she said.

"What you should do if something happens to me is just get out. Right away. Take Katy, don't stop for anything else, and go straight to your mother's."

"Do you think I'm so stupid I wouldn't know—"

"It's just best to have a plan," he went on doggedly. "Once you're at your mother's, call Harry and let him handle the details."

"And Katy and I will get your insurance and live happily ever after. The end."

"I'm serious, Judith."

"You're *too* serious. Go to sleep." She kissed him.

"Just don't do anything stupid," he said, reluctant to stop.

"When have I ever?"

Simon interrupted her routine half a dozen times a day. Judith would start outside and then stop with her hand on the doorknob, remembering he was out there. She would put off whatever she had planned to do outside until later. That's why she was even gladder when something else came along to occupy her thoughts.

One afternoon from his study Grey heard her answer the phone. The tone of her voice brought him into the living room. By then the call was ending and Judith was her calm, serious self. The caller probably had no idea how happy she was.

"I'm sure we can work something out. Goodbye, Mr. Rhodes."

She turned in Grey's direction and laughed, a rising, two-note laugh of triumph.

"Your boss at the bank?" Grey said, wondering how the old man could have made her this elated. "What'd he do, offer you a job?"

"Of sorts."

She told him. The bank was moving to a new building, and Mr. Rhodes wondered if, as a personal favor to him, Judith would "do" his new office.

"He liked my old office a lot, and he remembered that when I left the bank that's what I said I wanted to do someday."

Grey was ready to be happy for her, but he wanted to get all the facts straight. "What exactly does he want you to do?"

"Everything. Furniture, paintings, the filing cabinets—"

"Paper clips?"

"Especially the paper clips."

It was time for congratulations. Grey knocked off for the day and then broke out the best bottle of wine they had, drinking it from champagne glasses for the effect. Katy stood in the middle of the living room looking back and forth seriously between them, sensing her parents' mood. When one of them drank Katy would raise her hand for a taste, but she wasn't insistent.

"This is great." Judith's voice had lost its playfulness, if not its joy. Her voice was hard-edged, and her eyes ranged across the future. "There's a lot of traffic through Mr. Rhodes's office. Important traffic. If some of them like it, and if they ask who did it . . ."

"I thought you weren't going to start this until Katy was in school."

"I'm only talking about one job."

"Sounds like you're talking about a lot of jobs." Grey smiled, but Judith answered him seriously.

"If the opportunity comes now, I've got to take it. Besides, I might lose all my taste if I wait four or five years."

Grey was glad the call had come. In the following days Judith lost the fretful look he'd sometimes seen when she drifted through the days. The coffee table became cluttered with catalogs and sample books. The house was clearly one in which two working people lived. Judith made trips into town and steady phone calls. She might have been furnishing a building. The new offices were in the final stage of construction, and Judith went into Austin three times the first week to check on their progress.

Katy did not go neglected. Sometimes she stayed home with Grey, sometimes she accompanied her mother. "I think she's going to be a contractor," Judith told Grey.

Grey emerged from the kitchen on the Monday afternoon following the phone call from Mr. Rhodes. Counting them off on his fingers, he said, "We need coffee, and milk, and some kind of cereal, and . . . Do you want to go to the store, or shall I?"

"What?" Judith raised her distracted gaze from the catalog she was memorizing.

"I'll go," Grey said.

"Would you? I would, but I'm waiting for a call from Mr. Rhodes."

"I'll take Katy. Come on, Katy." The baby came running, as she always did whenever anyone went near a door. "Bye-bye," she said, meaning she wanted to go. Grey picked her up and went to the door. Judith heard it close, then open again. Grey stepped back in and called, "Lock the back door, why don't you? Judith?"

"I will," she called, not looking up. She heard Grey close and lock the front door. He passed in front of the window, and when she looked up to wave at him she saw the reason for his precaution. Simon was across the road.

He always was, of course. Judith had been neglecting him in her thoughts the past few days, but Simon had remained faithful. She wondered if he could sense that she'd been paying him less attention. Judith saw the car come slowly out of the driveway, pause there for a moment obscuring Simon, then move off, revealing Simon again behind a dust cloud. The man seemed unaffected by it. Judith went back to work.

A few minutes later the phone rang. She answered with alacrity, then stood frowning. "Well, when *can* we start?" she asked, after which her end of the conversation was limited to: "I see . . . Fine . . . Yes, I will . . . All right, good-bye."

She stood frowning over the replaced receiver, then told herself, "Get used to it, kid." Delays were probably inevitable in the business she'd chosen. Was choosing.

She slowly crossed the room, eyes down, face moving a bit. When she became aware of her surroundings again she was at the window. She looked out, frowned, moved slowly away.

Into the hall at the front door and along it to the kitchen, where she hurried her steps slightly to reach the window. The view was empty. She stepped to the door, locked it quickly, and smiled at her brief panic. The panes in the back door gave a slightly different view from the one from the window. She looked obliquely through them, thinking for a moment she saw something disappearing around the corner of the house.

Both the doors were locked. Judith fell back into her reverie, but when she returned to the living room she looked out the front window again, then moved to the side one. Her frown deepened. She walked back and across the short hall into Grey's study. There was only one window in there, and she stood at it for some time, moving from side to side to widen her view. It did no good. She left the room and made another quick circuit of all the ground-floor windows. There was no sign of Simon from any of them.

It was too early in the day for him to retire.

Maybe he had tried to follow Grey, but that would have been stupid. Aloud she said, "He's just trying to drive me crazy." And doing a fine job of it. She stood in front of the sofa, staring at the spot where she'd last seen him. There was no hiding place anywhere across the road.

Judith brought herself out of her trance with a resolute look. She strode across the living room and into the alcove behind the front door. She reached for the knob, but then stopped abruptly. Keeping her breath quiet, she leaned forward and put her eye to the peephole.

Nothing. But the peephole's angles gave a very limited view. She couldn't even tell if there was someone directly below it, crouched there less than a foot from her. She made sure the door was locked, and backed away from it.

Once more around all the windows. There was nothing to be seen from any of them. But they all offered the same problem. Even as a composite, they didn't give her a full view of the area around the house. She'd have to go outside for that.

After a while, standing so close to all those windows, trying to peer around their edges, left her feeling still less safe. So thin a protection, glass. She left the kitchen, keeping an eye on the windows until she was around the doorway.

In the living room she realized the solution. The stairs. Upstairs was the perspective she sought. From the terrace she'd be able to see almost all the surrounding country, and would be able to look down the walls of the house. Simon would look silly lurking there if she were looking directly down on him. She might even make some deprecating remark.

She was instantly calm again as she started up the stairs. There was nothing to fear, anyway. If their ragged watcher could make her this nervous just by not being around, then she wasn't very stable to begin with. She took the stairs jauntily, her heels tapping.

Upstairs, in the interior hallway, the house became her own again. Here she was as deep inside as she could get, with no thin walls of glass through which she could be spied on. She trailed a hand possessively along the wall as she crossed the hallway into the game room.

The doors to the terrace were open.

Panic returned immediately. Judith knew they never left those doors open, not since Katy's caper on the wall. She hurried toward them, then stopped. It was already too late. He was inside. She threw a frightened glance around the small room, seeing nothing unusual.

She had been a fool to think herself secure. It must be easy for a man to clamber up to the terrace, using a rope or a drainpipe. This house was little more than a lean-to, with too many openings to keep track of.

He was behind her.

He wasn't, but as soon as she spun around, feeling his presence directly behind her, she felt it again, still nearby, though the room had been empty a second before. She jumped forward, two quick steps bringing her to the hall door.

She looked out and saw nothing. Her bedroom door stood open next to her. She hurried through the door and slammed it, leaning her weight on it, expecting the thudding impact of a body hurling itself against the other side. Her scrabbling fingers got the door locked before that could happen. She sighed and backed away from the door.

But that was stupid. She had seen too many movies in which stupid victims backed into the arms of monsters. She whirled around and faced the room. She stooped to look under the bed, staying close enough to the door to be out it in an instant. The bed hid nothing but dust balls.

The closet door was open. She approached it slowly. Darkness within, clothes hanging and shoes on the floor. She looked at the shoes closely, trying to see if a pair of legs rose out of any of them. The closet was dark, but not very big. She crept toward it. The closer she got, the emptier of strangers it seemed, emboldening her to come still closer. Finally she stood between the open double doors and thrust her hands inside, all the way back into the corners. Her fingers touched the reassuring walls. After that she even jumped to look at the two shelves above her head. That was easier to bring herself to do: a man hiding up there couldn't possibly reach her before she would have time to be out the door and down the stairs. She already felt halfway there. A dream image of herself was hurtling down the stairs toward the free outdoors. It would take only an instant to join herself to that image. Adrenaline made her feet light.

She was safe now from everything except the bathroom. Its door stood ajar. Judith sidled along the wall to approach it. Her ears strained toward the hall door. She was still expecting impact there. Mentally, she had an eye on the closer of the two bedroom windows. She could see herself going through it at the first loud noise, in free fall, droplets of shattered glass outlining her body, the ground looming. The fall wouldn't kill her. But if it disabled her, that would be just as bad.

She was beside the bathroom door. Through the crack between the hinges she could see the small room. The mirror above the sink showed her the whole room, empty. But she had to go in. There was one more possibility, and this bedroom wouldn't be a sanctuary until she'd made absolutely sure. She stepped lightly onto the tile and approached the shower. She almost turned back then, but there was nothing outside the bathroom except that threatening hall door. She took a deep breath, as quietly as she could, and yanked open the shower curtain.

Grey found her quivering when he came home. She lay on the bed, hearing the door open, his voice calling, his footsteps approaching her hiding place. He knocked and called her name several times before she dragged herself up and stood behind the bedroom door.

"Grey?"

"Judith? Open the door. What's the matter?"

She had an instant of terrible regret as soon as she had turned the lock, but the next instant it was all right. Grey was there with Katy in his arms. Judith stood pale and strained in front of them, her hands limp on her thighs. Grey set Katy down and the baby wandered into the bedroom, talking wordlessly.

Grey held Judith's arms, supporting her. She gave the impression of falling. "What happened? Judith? Come sit down."

She was looking past him into the hallway. "Where is he?" she asked. Her voice grew stronger. "Did you see him?"

"Where? Here? He came in the house?" Grey's agitation was immediate. He stepped back toward the hall door and called for Katy.

Judith, by contrast, seemed very calm, emptied of blood and emotion. Grey came back to her and took hold of her arms. "What—" He thought of a dozen terrible things. "What did he do?"

Judith took a deep breath, and turned the exhalation into a laugh. "Nothing. I never even saw him. I came and locked myself in."

"How do you know he was here?"

Judith told him. By the end of the story she was up, moving around, straightening Katy's clothes. "It's working," she concluded. "He's trying to drive me crazy and he's succeeding."

Grey was silent. The strain that had left Judith's face had settled on his. Judith's voice grew concerned again when she looked at him.

"Oh, don't worry about it so much, Grey. Nothing happened. I don't really even know if he was up here, it could have been my imagination."

Grey forced his voice past an obstruction in his throat. "I didn't leave that terrace door open."

"Maybe I did. Or the wind. Really, stop it. I just scared myself because I'm so used to seeing him. It won't happen again."

"No. I'm not going to leave you alone here again and I'm going to talk to the police right now," he said.

"Please don't. I'm the one they'd want to talk

to and I'd just make a fool of myself. When they ask me what he did, all I could tell them is that he was outside and then he went away. That'll make them leap into action," she said with a wry smile.

Grey was silent. Soon he would force himself to smile, to reassure her, but he couldn't bring himself to do it yet.

"I'm sure he's harmless," Judith said, but her voice wasn't sure.

"This is shit," Simon said.

"No it isn't, honey. You're doing fine."

It was dusk in the ramshackle house in the woods. Waylon turned on a floor lamp. In the sudden brightness, Marcie was revealed standing beside Simon, stroking his arm. Simon stared out the grimy window as if expecting pursuit.

"It's going fine," Marcie repeated. "You've just got to keep the pressure on them. They're gonna crack like old clay."

"It's gittin' me nowhere."

"Yes it is. Just because you can't see it doesn't mean nothing's happening. I'll bet she wet her pants when she saw that door was open."

She had hoped that would draw a laugh from him. It drew only a shrug, but that was the friendliest response she'd gotten yet.

"Tell him, Waylon. Tell him he's doing fine."

"I think it's stupid," Waylon said quickly. He was pacing behind the sofa, the wheelchair in a corner. "This ain't doin' shit for him. That money's gone."

"Shut up," Simon told him. "You don't know anything." Marcie watched him carefully. "I'm getting my money," Simon said emphatically.

"That's right, honey." Marcie patted his arm again. "Well, I've got to get going, myself. I'd like to stay, but I'm still a schoolgirl, you know." She glanced at Waylon, who turned away. "I've got to be in school tomorrow. I'll see you in a couple of days. Okay, honey? Okay?" She stood behind Simon's shoulder until he grunted.

"Gimme a lift into town," he said suddenly, turning as she did.

Marcie looked at him uncertainly. "I don't think you better come home with me."

"I ain't."

"How will you get back?" she said hesitantly.

Simon walked past her and out the door. She heard her car door slam. "I guess he'll manage," she said. She looked at Waylon with a slight pout. He nodded, and watched her until she was out the door.

He had Marcie drop him off near the university. Simon didn't know where to find what he wanted, but he thought that would be the neighborhood to start looking. Marcie looked surprised when he stepped out of the car before she parked. Simon heard the car hesitate as he walked away from it. Marcie had seemed to believe he was planning to come home with her in spite of what he'd said. But Marcie wasn't what Simon had in mind tonight. He heard her call to him, then heard a car horn, finally heard Marcie's car rejoin the flow of traffic. He kept walking.

The night wasn't dark yet. Simon wore his boots, black pants, and a white shirt with flaps on the pockets and snaps instead of buttons, its sleeves rolled up. He walked with his head down, rubbing a hand over his cheeks and jaw. The sidewalk took him past apartment buildings and offices to an area of small shops. Beyond the shops was a bar. Not the one he wanted, but Simon went in anyway. He nursed a beer at the bar until a large, soft man in a soft-colored suit rose from a booth and went into the men's room. Simon finished his beer and followed him in.

The two of them were alone in the men's room. Simon stood at the urinal until the man emerged from the stall. They didn't glance at each other. The man went to the sink behind Simon, studied his own eyes in the mirror, then stooped to splash water on his face.

Simon stepped quickly to the man, grasped

the back of his neck, and slammed his forehead down on the porcelain. The man, stunned, struggled upward. This time Simon whisked the man's feet from under him as he slammed his head down again. The combined forces loosened the sink in its moorings and left the stranger unconscious, facedown on the floor.

Simon went quickly through the man's pockets, cursed when he found nothing in the wallet, but grunted with satisfaction when he discovered a fold of bills in another pocket. He dropped it in his shirt pocket without counting; a glance had shown him it would be more than enough to finance his evening. Simon left the man where he lay and stepped briskly out the door, his head down again. He turned away from the well-lighted barroom, went down a short hallway to the kitchen and through it to the alley. No one said anything to him.

He moved in no hurry. In the next hour he forgot where his money had come from. In that time he dropped into several bars, having whiskey now, staying just long enough to meet a few eyes and look the places over. In one place he was approached by a short, dark woman, but he wasn't interested. He didn't find what he did want, and it made him surly. One of several things Simon had learned in prison was patience, but in prison he'd had nothing to drink. Liquor made his wants more immediate.

He found what he was looking for in a little neighborhood bar just dingy enough to make him feel comfortable. She was standing at a table of three men, talking as if she knew them, and one of the men said something to the other two that made them laugh. Simon sat at the bar and studied her. She was way over-dressed for her setting in a long, dark dress. She wore it to look slender, and almost succeeded. In high school she was probably a beautiful girl, but high school was more than twenty years behind her. Her business hours had been hard on her complexion, but the dim bar light was kind to it. From a certain distance and a certain alcohol-softened critical perspective she was still beautiful. To Simon, who had no experience at all with the kind of woman he was looking for, she looked like just what he wanted: a tall cool blonde with a haughty look. Peering at her through half-closed eyes he imagined he was catching glimpses of her through a picture window, or more exposed in a swimming pool, her legs moving palely in the water.

But her voice ruined the illusion. She worked her way down the bar to him slowly. One man bought her a drink but nothing more. She had finished it by the time she sat down beside Simon and said, "Hi, honey. If you insist on buyin' me a drink I'd be too polite to refuse it."

"Leave him alone, Alice," the bartender said casually.

"It's all right," Simon said.

"Yeah, it's all right. We're old pals. Wanta buy an old pal a drink, honey?"

Simon nodded minutely and the bartender went away to make her usual.

She chatted to Simon about the weather for a few minutes. Her voice grated on him. From up close he wasn't so satisfied with her appearance, either. But when she neared the bottom of her drink and said, "Wanta go someplace quiet where we can talk, honey?" he thought she was as close a substitute as he was likely to find tonight. He looked at her silently for a minute. The way he stared made her think she might be making a mistake.

"If you think you can shut the hell up for an hour," he finally said.

"Me? I'm a dummy, I'm a deaf mute." She pantomimed zipping her lip.

"All right," Simon said, and left money on the bar. He took her arm above the elbow, a little too tightly, and they walked out.

They were barely out the door when she was yanked out of Simon's grip. "Hey," she said angrily. It was one of the guys from the table, the joke-teller.

"Thought you weren't going to do this anymore," he said to Alice.

"Well, Frank, I just thought I would between engagements on my concert tour. Whattaya want me to do, starve to death?"

"You don't have to do this," Frank said in a low voice.

"She does right now," Simon said, reaching between them to take her hand.

"Just stay out of it, pal, this has nothing to do with you." Frank hadn't even looked at him. He was embarrassed. He wore a wedding ring.

"You're the one it's got nothin' ta do with. Why don't you fuck off and let us get about our business?"

Frank looked at him in surprise. Simon grabbed the woman's arm again and turned. Frank pushed him away from her. When Simon turned back again Frank had his hands up, half-curled into fists. Frank was heavy in the belly but also in the arms, and he looked ready to fight if he had to.

"I don't want to hurt you, pal," he said.

That was his mistake. Because this was the other thing Simon had been looking for, without realizing it. Liquor had brought his frustration to the surface. He badly wanted to hurt someone.

He put up his hands placatingly and took a step back. "Come on, Frank," the blonde said. "Don't do this. Act your age."

She laid a hand on one of Frank's raised

arms, trying to force it back down. Frank shook off her hand and turned to her irritably.

Simon struck. He stepped between Frank's hands and lifted his knee into the man's crotch.

The movement returned Frank's attention to Simon. He shifted to avoid the blow, but Simon's knee still caught one thigh, throwing Frank off balance. One of Frank's fists cut the air, but Simon stepped inside it and hammered him in the face. The blow shook Frank loose from his vision for a moment.

Frank scrambled upright and struck out blindly. His hand hit Simon's jaw and slid to his mouth. Simon bit down.

The woman was saying, "Stop, stop," and ineffectually trying to separate them. Frank was down on his knees, clinging to Simon's legs, trying to drag him down. Simon dropped on top of him and while his knees dug into Frank's chest Simon hit him as hard as he could with each fist. The fury on his face made Alice back away. She stood in the shadows of the building, staring.

Simon sprang up and glared around. "There you are." He grabbed her arm again. Alice shrank from the contact.

"Come on," Simon said. "We got a date, don't we?"

Alice resisted. "Frank?" she said. The man

on the ground was stirring slightly. His chest heaved.

"Come on!" Simon said again.

"Okay, honey, okay." She was trying to get her footing.

"And shut the hell up," he reminded her. Simon put his arm around her and dragged her along the sidewalk. After a few steps she stopped resisting.

# 9

MOWING THE GRASS OUT HERE IN THE COUNTRY was a different proposition from doing it in town. There was none of the suburban camaraderie, waving to neighbors out mowing their own lawns on a Saturday, stopping to chat. Here Grey was a pioneer—man against the wilderness, armed only with a lawn mower. He felt a little silly. Grass grew rampant for miles around, yet he was going to hold it at bay from this one small plot of civilization. But there was a matter of pride too. The grass might someday grow tall and wild around this house, but it would have to wait until he no longer laid claim to it.

Shortly after Grey started, Simon came ambling down the road. There was a bend in the road less than half a mile away, and Grey saw him coming soon after Simon made that turn. He didn't have the dog or the gun with him today, but he wore a loose jacket that could have hidden several weapons. Grey watched him come as he mowed the length of one row of grass, and didn't like to turn his back on Simon as he mowed the next one. Grey was remembering the way Judith had been left trembling at the thought of Simon in the house. She had tried to convince him that it had just been her imagination, but neither of them was sure of that. Simon looked sleepy and not very attentive this morning as he took up his post across the road, but he watched Grey curiously, giving up his usual pretense of looking everywhere except at the house and its occupants. His gaze made Grey self-conscious. Simon was dressed in old black pants, boots, and his customary hat. He needed a shave and his hair was unruly. Grey, on the other hand, wore faded red gym shorts, thongs, and a T-shirt that said "Everything's New in Quintana Roo." His legs were bare and his hair combed. He felt as if he and Simon were part of a Smithsonian exhibit portraying the evolution of man. But the emotions Grey felt were primitive. His hands tightened on the handles of the mower. As soon as he finished the front yard he went inside to his family.

The next day Grey was back outside to mow the backyard, but this time he had the bulk of the house to protect him from the scrutiny of Simon, who was already sitting across the road in front. Grey had the sprinkler going in the front yard, throwing up a very thin screen between Simon and the house.

Mowing in the back was an even more arbitrary business than mowing the front yard. In the front the road and the driveway marked the boundaries of Grey's property, but in the back there were no markers. He could mow as far as he wanted. Mowing was a way of claiming territory.

He found that he did some of his best thinking during times like this, when his body was occupied with a monotonous task and his mind was free to roam. Today he found himself thinking about the beginnings of the jury system, when in the Middle Ages juries were composed of people somehow involved in the case at hand—witnesses, relatives. If a man had no interest in a case, why should he listen to it? Only the involved or the injured would be passionate enough to seek justice.

He could not fail to remain aware of Simon. Grey could see the watcher every time he came to the end of mowing a row, when he got far enough to the side to see past the house to Simon across the street in front. The man was always there. Grey glanced at him first from one side of the house, then a minute later from the other side.

Still preoccupied with his thoughts, he came to the end of a row, turned the mower, and felt something out of place. He looked at the house. There was nothing to be seen there. Judith and the baby had both been upstairs when he'd come outside. Judith wasn't at any of the windows.

He came to the end of the next row and looked across the street, but didn't see Simon. Simon must have shifted to the side. Grey pushed the mower faster and craned his head forward to see around the other corner of the house. He drew level with that corner and could see across the street from another angle, but there was still no sign of Simon. Grey kept walking, enlarging his view of the area across the road from the front of the house. He was mowing a narrow finger of mowed grass into the grass that had never been mowed, the wild grass that grew as high as his knees. He could see the spot where Simon had been sitting, but he wasn't there now. Simon could have hidden from view by walking in the opposite direction from Grey, keeping the house between them, but why would he do that? There hadn't been time for him to get out of sight in any other direction. If he had walked off down the road or across the fields, Grey would have seen him. A car could have come along the road and picked him up, but Grey hadn't noticed a car. The only place Simon could have gone to stay out of sight—

The lawn mower sputtered and died. Grey left it and walked quickly back across the yard. By the time he reached the house he was running. He felt silly but it would take only a moment to reassure himself. Distractedly he grabbed the knob of the back door.

His shoulder banged into the door. It was locked. Grey twisted the knob hard and pushed, thinking it was just stuck, but the doorknob wouldn't budge.

That was all wrong. He wouldn't have locked himself out. He peered through the glass of the back door. The kitchen was empty and that was all he could see. The interior of the house was dim, even in the kitchen with its big window.

Grey backed up, staring up the walls of the house. No lights blossomed in the windows. "Judith?" Grey called. All the windows were closed, the air conditioner running. He started to run around to the front door, but he knew it was locked, he would only waste time.

"Judith!" he shouted much more loudly. When there was no response he shouted again, and then again.

Her face appeared at an upstairs window, pressed against the glass. Grey signaled frantically and she raised the window. There could have been a man standing behind her.

"Are you all right?" he shouted.

"Yes." Something wrong with her voice.

"The door's locked. Come down and let me in. Be careful," he added, shouting, but she had already disappeared.

He walked back to the door. Simon could be in the hall, waiting for her, or on the stairs. Grey could have just sent her right into the trap. He twisted the knob back and forth, jittering. The kitchen remained empty. Judith wouldn't be able to hear him now unless he shouted. Would he be able to hear her scream? He could almost hear it, like the memory of a scream.

Too much time had passed. "Judith?" Grey called again. He looked around for something to break the glass in the door. There were no tools. The heaviest thing around was the lawn mower, but it was back there in the tall grass. There were four brick paving stones used as steps, embedded in the ground leading away from the back door. He was frantically prying one up with his fingers when the back door opened.

Grey looked up. Judith was standing there, but he still wanted the reassuring weight of the brick in his hands, in case she wasn't alone.

"What are you doing?" she asked.

Grey stood up and took her arm. She looked at his muddy hand distastefully. "Are you all right?" he asked.

"Of course. What's wrong with you?"

"Why didn't you have on any lights?"

"I was lying down," she said irritably. "Is

that all right with you? I'm sorry I'm not as industrious as you—"

Grey was still holding the brick. There seemed no need for it, so he dropped it to the ground. Judith looked at him, looked at the brick, and getting no response, she knelt herself and carefully placed the brick back in the depression from which he had dug it.

"Why did you lock the back door?" he asked.

"I didn't," she said shortly, still looking at him as if he had gone suddenly lunatic.

Grey could have locked the door himself when he went out. He had gotten in that habit. But he didn't remember doing so.

Judith stood up, brushing the dirt from her hands. He followed her into the kitchen, where she snapped on the overhead light. "There," she said. "Happy?"

"Where's Katy?"

"I put her in her playpen while I was coming to see what you wanted." Judith was still annoyed with him and he was a little mad at himself for getting so needlessly upset. It would almost have been better if there had been some danger.

There was a thump from the living room. Grey, already skittish, gave Judith a sharp look and hurried out of the kitchen. Judith followed more slowly, rolling her eyes. When she reached the living room Grey said to her, "You shouldn't leave her like this."

The thump had been a heavy glass ashtray falling to the floor when Katy pulled herself upright on the end table on which the ashtray had rested. The baby was standing near the front door, ten feet from the playpen.

"I didn't leave her like this," Judith said. "I left her in the playpen, like I told you."

They looked at each other. Katy hadn't yet been able to climb out of the playpen. She had to be lifted out.

"Bye-bye," Katy said to the door. Grey went and picked her up. She smiled at him. There was nothing wrong with her that he could see. She was such a happy child, even friendly to strangers. But a baby seemed so fragile. Grey sometimes thought he could look at her and see Katy's whole lifetime compressed down into her tiny frame. Any mark on her now would grow with time, like a scar. There were moments when there seemed to him no more dangerous an occupation than raising a baby, because anything that happened to her now could assume such significance through the rest of her life. Even toilet training seemed hazardous.

He hugged her and she put her arms around his neck, saying "Daddy" as if concerned about him. Grey walked to the picture window. The grass in the front yard gleamed wetly from the sprinkler. Across the road Simon sat in his original spot. His head moved slowly back and forth. Grey imagined that for an instant as their gazes crossed Simon's eye gleamed with amusement.

"Bastard," Grey said softly.

Judith had gone silent, watching Grey. He gave her the baby and went to the front door. It was locked, of course. Grey opened it and looked at the outside lock and doorknob, but couldn't tell anything. It wasn't a very good lock. A city burglar would laugh at it. But city burglars stayed in the city, and he hadn't imagined there was any thief out here with the sophistication to pick a lock.

Anyone crossing that front yard would have gotten his feet wet. There were no wet footprints inside the house, but the mat outside, which was protected by the porch roof and should have been dry, was wet. Grey stood up from feeling its dampness. Across the road, Simon was ostentatiously looking in another direction. Grey turned and saw Judith and Katy both watching him, Katy with a perfectly open, innocent expression.

"All right," Grey said. "That just about does it for me." He closed the door.

Grey guessed as soon as he saw the building that it had been built by the WPA. He was right. A small plaque on the front proclaimed the achievement, the erection in 1936 of the nondescript stone building. Two square stories, with bars on one window at the side, the bars newer than the building. They must have been added later, after people had decided that the building would be a sheriff's office. Grey pictured a team of men roving through the Depression, throwing up buildings with reckless abandon, so that the inhabitants had to come along later and find a use for them.

The sheriff's body, on the other hand, had clearly been built to house a sheriff. The man was beefy, heavy-armed, with a face that retained a certain authoritative menace even when he smiled. Grey found him without having to pass through an intervening secretary. The sheriff was typing something himself, on an old manual typewriter, and seemed glad of the distraction. When Grey introduced himself the sheriff stuck out his hand and said, "Jim Kendrick. How are ya doing?"

"Fine," Grey said inaccurately. For a minute it seemed like a social call. The glimpse through an open door behind the sheriff of the empty cell reminded Grey of his purpose. He outlined in a few words what had been happening. He'd planned to make the account longer, but as soon as he started talking all the incidents seemed trivial. The sheriff's face lost its sociability and dropped into an official neutrality.

The most emotion the sheriff displayed was when Grey mentioned Simon's name. The sheriff's mouth moved slightly before he said, "I know him."

Grey thought he detected sympathy in that response. "Well then," he said, and went on with the story. But when he finished Kendrick only looked at him as if there must be more.

"Do you want to file a complaint?" he said.

"Well—" Grey blinked. "I don't want to send the man back to prison. I just want him to leave us alone."

Kendrick shrugged one shoulder. "I'm sure you know how the law works. I want to help you, but you're the one who has to decide what to do." A silence started as they looked at each other, and the sheriff filled it. "Let me help you decide. All you've got to accuse him of is trespassing, right? And that only applies to the couple of times you've seen him cutting across your backyard, because nobody has actually seen him in the house, right?"

Grey nodded. Kendrick shrugged again.

"Now, if you want to file a complaint, I'll go get him. But it doesn't amount to much, and he'll probably be back in a day."

"I was just hoping you could do something to discourage him."

"Just want me to harass him, huh?" The sheriff grinned.

"That's what he's doing to us. My wife was terrified yesterday, and again this morning."

"I'm sorry," Kendrick said. "I know that

Hocksley's a mean bastard. I'll see what I can do."

"Thanks. What would you suggest I do in the meantime?" Grey didn't expect much useful advice and the sheriff didn't have any, though he clearly wanted to help. The visit trailed off in a few more sentences.

Grey emerged from the building into an overcast day. The low cloud ceiling made him feel tall, stretched between earth and sky. He didn't feel like going home yet. Judith was in Austin, Katy at Judith's mother's. As he'd promised, he wouldn't leave them alone in the house again. But he had time of his own now. He tried to think of a valuable use for it.

He was in an area unfamiliar to him, farther west of Austin from his house. It was a very small crossroads village, useful perhaps, but he'd never explored it. Their natural impulse when buying gas or groceries was to head toward Austin. Now he looked around. Broad spaces separated the few buildings: gas station, general store, deserted café. The newest building was a small real-estate office, but it looked closed.

He drove slowly to the store. It stood alone on the highway, as if it claimed extensive territorial rights. At night it would seem completely isolated, in spite of the relative nearness of the other buildings. Grey parked and went in.

The store was bigger than he'd supposed, but retained an old-fashioned flavor. The walls of the rectangular room were old dark boards, as was the long counter in front. There was a faded red metal Coke cooler, and the long shelves were well-stocked. The glass doors of the refrigerator case looked out of place. There were no humans in evidence.

The place looked familiar. Grey was trying to sort it out when, "Help you?" he heard behind him, and turned to see that a woman had taken her place behind the counter.

She looked familiar too. Slightly younger than Grey, she projected a disconcerting image of youth and experience. Her forehead, gleaming palely through the strands of hair that fell across it, dominated her face and gave her a practical look. She wore jeans and a gray T-shirt, the shirt emphasizing her shoulders rather than her breasts.

He had seen her somewhere other than this store. He must have been frowning as he tried to think of it, because she frowned slightly too when she said, "Can I do something for you?"

"I'm sorry. I was just . . . I've seen you before."

"Yes," she said, not warming up. Grey still looked puzzled. "In court," she said.

That didn't bring it back to him. "Were you a client?" he asked slowly, feeling he was on the verge of placing her. And this store, too . . . "Oh," he said. "Yes, now . . . This is the place he robbed."

She nodded without expression. Everyone was looking at him neutrally today.

"I'm sorry," he said. "That's . . . You're mad, aren't you?"

Her shrug was as good as a nod.

"You think I was trying to loose a mad dog back on society."

Her mouth twitched toward a smile and her shoulders became less defiant. "No, I know, you were just . . . It's just that I've had occasion lately to be reminded of the case."

"So have I," Grey said. "My client thinks I robbed him."

She raised her eyebrows, and he told her about Simon's campaign to regain his loot. He talked quickly, sensing her thawing. She was shaking her head when he finished. "Bastard," she muttered.

"Oh, it's probably nothing to worry about. The sheriff didn't seem to think so. After all, he hasn't—"

She leaned across the counter toward him, her face going hard again. "*I'd* worry."

Her tone stopped him. He looked at her closely. "I don't remember," he said slowly, "exactly what happened during the robbery. He wasn't armed, I don't think—"

"No. He didn't have to be. Do you want to

hear the story?" She was leaning on both arms on the counter. He thought for a moment she was trembling, but in fact she was very still, rigid. "I'll tell you exactly what happened, if you promise not to interrupt with objections this time." Her smile was tiny and brief.

"He came into the store that night. Hocksley. It was dark, there hadn't been a customer in an hour, I was thinking about closing early. He came wearing a mask, a bandanna, like a Western outlaw. I could tell who he was, though. He'd been in here before.

"Of course, I knew it was trouble right away, but robbery wasn't the first thing that occurred to me. Randy was in Austin and there was nobody around. He didn't say anything at first. I was trying to decide what to do, how to get out of it alive. I didn't even notice that he didn't have a gun.

"He didn't say anything, just came behind the counter and pushed me out of the way. I smelled liquor, like it had been poured on him. He tried to get the cash register open, but kept hitting the wrong buttons. I reached up to do it for him, but he knocked my hand away.

"He finally got it open and took the cash. Seventy, eighty dollars, I don't know. By then I was starting to think he'd just go away. But he put the money in his pocket and turned to me. I was back here in the corner. All I was thinking about was running, but I couldn't make myself start, it was like the walls were holding me in place.

"He came up to me, real slow, and just stood there. I was trying to shrink into the wall, and cover every part of my body at the same time. We stood there like that for a long time. I kept hoping someone would come in, or just drive by and scare him off. It looked like he was trying to decide whether or not to kill me.

"Then, real fast, his hand came up and grabbed my throat. Not very tight, just holding me there. I tried to grab his hand, but he put his other hand on my stomach and then started moving it around. So I tried to hold that one off instead."

Her voice was low, her face immobile, while Grey's face moved sympathetically; he flinched whenever something happened in the narrative. The woman's only reaction was to swallow more frequently.

"Then all of a sudden he tightened the hand on my throat. So fast I didn't have time to get a breath. So hard I thought he'd already crushed everything, that I was going to die, even if he let me go. I was trying to claw his hand away, but he was fighting me off with the other one. I tried to kick him, but I couldn't see, and he turned so I was just kicking the sides of his legs.

"I was dead. I couldn't see, I couldn't yell, I couldn't hear anything but my heart. I thought,

'He's killing me.' My last words. It was so stupid and obvious: 'He's killing me.'

"Then just as fast, he let go. He unclenched his hand and just held me in place. I was breathing again before I even realized I was still alive. It was like coming back from the dead. For a minute I couldn't remember what was happening or where I was. Then I saw his face in front of me and I remembered and I wished he'd let me die."

She was starting to show more emotion now. Her eyes widened and her breath came more quickly. She could still bring alive the surprise of that moment. "Why'd he do it?" Grey asked uneasily. For a wild moment he'd thought the woman was going to die now, in front of him.

She might have been answering his question or she might have been continuing her story: "He leaned close to me and said, 'There's more.' His breath was the only thing I could smell. I didn't know what he was talking about. He shook me a little and said, 'More money.'

"I was so happy! Because there was, there was more money. I was so happy I had something to give him. I started nodding like a crazy person, crying, pointing into the back. I tried to shout, 'I'll get it,' but it came out just a croak.

"He smiled—I could tell it from his eyes—and he let go of me and stepped back. All of a sudden he seemed real happy too. Happy for me! Because I'd said the right thing. Then we were both happy. It was like we'd suddenly become partners. And I was just glad to be alive. No matter how terrible it was, every minute seemed extra, you know?"

Grey nodded.

"So I took him into the back, leading him like we were in a cave together. I got the other money and gave it to him and watched while he counted it. I started smiling, because *he* was, because he seemed so pleased that there was more money."

"Was it much more?"

She nodded, said, "Yeah," and hurried on: "Then time started slowing down again. I watched him counting the last few bills and I realized that was the last thing I had, I didn't have anything else to give him if he asked me again. I almost started crying. I wanted to back away, or run, but I didn't want to do anything that would call his attention to me again. So I just stood there shaking and trying to be small. Watching his hands.

"He finished counting the money and looked up, smiling, and then he quit smiling, like he was surprised I was still there, and realized he had to do something."

She paused. "Then?" Grey asked gently.

"Then we heard a car outside, out in back. Randy getting home. For a second Hocksley and I looked at each other like conspirators. He actually put one finger up in front of his face, like 'Shhh,' you know, and I did the same thing. Then he turned around and ran, out the front, and I just stood there, not screaming or calling to Randy to hurry or going to see where he went. Just standing there."

That's what she did now: just stood, hands loosely at her sides, staring at a point behind Grey's head. He became aware of her breath, and of his. He hadn't heard either during the telling of the story.

"I'm sorry," he said.

She saw him again. "For what?" she said easily. "Getting him off? It didn't matter by then." Grey shrugged and so did she. He realized he hadn't told her his name, and did so.

"Grey? Kind of a funny name."

"My mother was a funny woman."

She smiled; some people did. "Lucinda Carmack," she said. "Sounds like I came right out of these hills, doesn't it? Name like that."

"Where did you come from?"

"D.C. Went to school at U.T., don't ask me why. Randy and I came out here almost ten years ago. When we were hippies." She said it dryly, as if it had been her major. "We were all getting back to the land. Our friends drifted back into town pretty fast, but we liked it, and I found out I was good at running a store."

"And Randy? Your husband?"

She nodded. "Well, Randy still has to go into Austin to work. He's a carpenter. Not much call for it around here.

"I could hardly get him to start leaving me here alone again after that night. I didn't want to tell him what happened, but he made me. It was easy to see—Randy wanted to go after him. I didn't want to do anything. I didn't want to make Hocksley mad. We compromised by calling the sheriff."

"The extra money you mentioned," Grey said, musing. "That didn't come up at the trial, did it? That's what you were so evasive about when you testified."

"That's how you made me look like a liar," Lucinda said calmly. She held up a hand to forestall his apology. "It was my own fault. Yeah, the extra money, that was our little nest egg. The IRS didn't know about and I didn't see why anyone else should."

Grey shook his head, uncomprehending. Lucinda was patient.

"Try to imagine where we could have come up with a fairly large chunk of illegal cash."

There were any number of explanations. The most obvious was drug sales. Lucinda had said she was a good businesswoman. Grey nodded, and she nodded along with him.

"Was it much?"

"You being an officer of the court, I'd rather

not discuss it. But it was a pretty good sum. Simon would have thought so, especially."

"What does he do?" Grey asked. The bell on the door of the store tinkled, and they turned quick stares in that direction. A man in a fishing hat hurried inside and went directly toward the beer case at the back of the store.

"Anything," Lucinda answered Grey's question. "He and his brother have a few acres, raise a little. Do a few odd jobs once in a while for the other farmers around. I'd bet they don't see two thousand dollars in cash in a year."

Grey absorbed that information while the fisherman stepped around him, paid for his beer, and left. Lucinda, watching the car pull out of the parking lot, said, "And now he's bothering you?"

After hearing her story, his own problems seemed petty. Grey shrugged deprecatingly. "Yeah, well . . . he's just hanging around. He hasn't really done anything to worry about. The sheriff—"

"The sheriff goes way back with the Hocksleys, but he doesn't know Simon as well as I do after one encounter. Look . . ." She leaned across the counter as if imparting secret information. "You think because a thing looks something like you and uses English that it's human, but you're wrong. He is an animal. You try to remember that."

She was marked by her experience. Grey nodded soberly, and asked another question.

"Didn't you say you'd been reminded of it recently? Why?"

Lucinda looked at him flatly. "He came in the store. A few days after he got out. I'd already heard, I figured he might come by."

"What did he want?"

"I don't know. I didn't give him a chance to ask."

Grey looked a question. Lucinda looked out the window, and Grey followed her gaze. The parking lot and the road were empty. Grey turned back when he sensed movement. Lucinda's hand came from under the counter and she dropped the heavy object there. Grey stepped aside out of its line: a big, old revolver, black with age, heavy with menace. Grey looked at it. Lucinda looked at him.

"I showed him this. Had it in my hand before he even stepped inside. When he did I pointed it straight at him and told him the truth: nothing would make me happier than to blow his fucking head off, and if he ever came near me again I'd do it."

Her voice stayed firm, but passion filled its undertones. Grey was looking at the pistol as if it had spoken. Lucinda moved slowly and put it away again, glancing out the windows. "He left," she said shortly.

"You seem to know how to handle him."

Lucinda looked at him to see if he was being ironic. Satisfied he wasn't, she said calmly, "I'm scared to death of him. But I would kill him. I'd love to."

Grey was ready to ease himself out of the conversation. "I think I'll try to find some other way," he said, and moved away into the shelves. He picked out a few things while Lucinda watched. After he'd paid and had hefted the two sacks into his arms, she stopped him. He was leaning back against the door, almost gone.

"Before I met you today," she said, "I'd been almost hoping Simon would do something to someone bad enough to get sent back to prison for a long time. But I wouldn't want anything to happen to you or your family." She looked down, slightly embarrassed. "You just be careful, that's all I'm saying."

"I will," Grey said seriously, and went out the door, in a hurry to get home before Judith did.

# 10

JUDITH CAME IN THE BACK DOOR WITH HER ARMS full, said "Damn" when she dropped a roll of sample fabrics, then said it again every time something else fell. Four damns by the time she dumped the remainder on the sofa and went back for the spills. The back door stood open. She pushed it to, dropped the spilled rolls on the sofa with the rest, and went upstairs.

Shower water beat on her comfortingly. For long minutes she stood with eyes closed, not reaching for the soap or shampoo, letting the forceful droplets attack her tired muscles. She began to feel that she would live through the day.

A distant noise made her feel suddenly naked. Funny how you didn't in your own shower alone in the house. But as soon as there was a possibility of someone nearby . . . Judith held her head high above the shower, trying to will the water quiet. She couldn't hear anything above it. Or maybe she could, but her imagination was running by then and she couldn't trust her ears.

There was no sense trying to go on with her shower. She stepped out, feeling even more naked in the air. She left the water running for its protective sound and diversion. Reaching for her robe hanging on a hook behind the door, she hurriedly dried her feet with a towel. She didn't want to leave footprints.

Her throat tightened as she stepped out the door. This was the bedroom he'd trapped her in once before, and this time she knew there could be no one hiding in the shower. It would be easy to reach the door and lock it, but she wasn't going to be put through that again. The tiny sounds struggling to emanate from her throat were more growl than whimper. Judith quietly opened the closet door and fumbled through it for a weapon. Grey had an old set of golf clubs, but he kept them downstairs. Why didn't they keep a baseball bat up here, or a gun? She finally settled for an umbrella with a sharp point. She held it in front of her as she stalked across the room. She pushed the point out the door ahead of her and followed it with great caution, looking both ways up and down the hall.

The silence was unbroken upstairs, but as she stood there she heard another sound from below. Taking a firmer grip on the umbrella, she moved swiftly and quietly to the head of the stairs. Drops fell to the rug from under her robe. Her feet were already wet again. She almost slipped when she touched the first bare step.

Her fear was translating into anger, and she grew madder and madder as she came down. She took the last of the stairs in a rush, and raised the umbrella high. She would be glad to put it through his eye. She pictured his face falling into fright as she lunged at him. Let him be the fearful one for a change.

He was in the kitchen, coming toward her. She'd forgotten to lock the door, but now she was glad of it. She lunged through the doorway, arms back, the point of the umbrella above her head, poised to come down hard.

Grey almost walked straight into it. Katy, in his arms, shrieked. Judith dropped the umbrella and it took both of them to convince Katy it had been a game. "Mommy," Katy kept saying reprovingly. Grey glared at Judith every time he looked up. Between soothing sentences to Katy he said, "What the hell were you doing?"

"I'm sorry," Judith said unapologetically. "I thought it was him. I was taking a shower and I heard something. Why didn't you *say* something?" she added accusingly.

"I heard the water running and I *assumed*

that's where you were. I didn't know you were creeping down the stairs armed to kill."

"I'm sorry. I said I was sorry, what do you want?" Katy, no longer concerned, was walking around the floor. Grey and Judith had assumed the strain. They stood tensely, several steps apart. Judith began to pace. "I never feel safe here anymore. It doesn't even matter anymore if he's out there. Look. Is he out there now? If he's not, that's worse, because then we don't know *where* he is, or what he's doing."

"What do you want me to do about it?" Grey's voice was as tight as hers. "I've done everything I can, short of shooting him. Is that what you want? Besides, I told you not to stay here by yourself anymore."

"I know, but we finished early and Mr. Rhodes . . . Anyway . . ." She stopped explaining and clawed her hair back from her face. "Where the hell am I supposed to go if I get here and you're not here? Turn around and go back to Austin?"

"I'll show you," Grey said, and took her hand.

Lucinda took to Judith with a quickness that suggested a lack of company in her life, and Judith was flatteringly attentive in return. Grey took his wife's expression to mean he had brought her to an interesting curiosity, but Lucinda couldn't tell she was being patronized.

Judith lost her detachment when she asked about Lucinda's encounter with Simon. Lucinda launched into the story enthusiastically. Grey had sketched it out for Judith already, but standing at the scene of the crime and listening to the victim revived Judith's sense of horror. Perhaps she was projecting herself into Lucinda's place.

"Grey," she called. "Have you heard all this?"

Grey nodded, but the women weren't paying any attention to him. Katy had delightedly assumed ownership of the store. He followed her around the aisles, keeping breakables away from her and restoring order in her wake. He had wanted Judith and Lucinda to like each other, but they had become so thick so quickly that he felt excluded. "But I'm worried about *you,*" he heard Lucinda say.

"Oh, no. Nothing like so terrible a thing has happened to *us*. And I really don't think—"

"You shouldn't take it so lightly. I was telling your husband, if it were me I'd . . ."

With Katy's guidance, Grey explored the store more thoroughly than he had on his first visit. One corner was devoted to hardware. Katy stopped there, reaching for the small packages hanging on hooks.

"No, no. Mustn't play with nails."

Katy was insistent. He picked her up and

offered a few safe packages for her inspection. That kept her occupied long enough for Grey to find something that interested him: a display of deadbolt locks. He examined them as well as he could through their hard plastic packaging and finally carried three to the front counter. Lucinda didn't interrupt her conversation with Judith while she moved to the cash register and rang up the sale. Grey waited patiently a few more minutes, and finally almost had to drag Judith away. Lucinda let her go only after a promise to return soon.

"Didn't you think she was interesting?" Judith said in the car, which was more than she'd said to him on the trip *to* the store.

"Remember why I brought you here. That's where I want you to go if I'm ever not home. It's close to our house and she's got a gun."

"I know. She said she'd kill him, but I don't think she would, do you? What did you buy?" She opened the sack and said, "Locks?"

"Good locks," Grey said. "One for the front door, one for the back, and one for the terrace doors."

There were two or three hours of sun left when they got home, and Grey went to work. He stood outside the front door, satisfied to see Simon nowhere around. The lock was a satisfying weight in his hand, a simple, solid mechanism. They were good locks, deadbolts that couldn't be forced or picked except by someone much more expert than anyone likely to be found in this area. They might even hold against a bullet. An intruder would have to smash down the door itself to get in. The front door was sturdy enough to resist assault. The back door had too many glass panes in it, but it would do a burglar no good to break one pane near the lock. Inside and out, the lock could only be opened with a key. He had even bought one for the terrace doors upstairs. Judith came out to watch him work as he was installing that one, the final lock.

"What if these don't work?" she said. "Are you going to add a new lock every week? This will start to look like a New York apartment."

"These will do it," Grey said, satisfied. He gave a final strong twist to a screw and stood up. "Done."

"Very nice," Judith said. "I feel all safe and warm now." She smiled slightly.

"I'll pretend not to hear the sarcasm in that. I feel like I've done a good day's work. And look—" He took her out on the terrace and made a sweeping gesture. "He's nowhere around. The locks work like a charm. I feel like celebrating. Let's eat out."

Judith yawned. "I don't feel like driving back into Austin."

"Would you rather cook? . . . I thought so. I was going to suggest we try that place across the road from Lucinda's store. She said it's not bad. People come from miles around."

"That's because there's nothing else *for* miles around."

"Exactly. Let's get cleaned up."

"I don't like it," Waylon said to Marcie.

"But, honey, I've got to stay close to him. How else am I going to find out what he knows?" She laughed at him. "I didn't know you were the jealous type."

He hated being teased, and she knew it. Moodily Waylon walked to the window and looked out at the darkening emptiness. He expected Simon to return any minute. He always expected Simon's return. Marcie came to stand behind him, and sank her chin on his shoulder. "Don't worry. Everything's going fine. As soon as this is over we can go to work and make some money. I've had my eye on a little antique store that's all alone on the highway—"

"I hate it," Waylon said. "All I'm doin' is waitin'."

She turned him around and slipped her arms under his. After a few sullen moments he responded. "Don't worry," she said again. "You won't have to wait much longer."

The door slammed back against the wall when Simon came through it. Marcie and Waylon had leaped apart a moment before when they'd heard his heavy step on the porch. Simon only gave them one angry glare and then turned his attention to various cabinets around the room, rummaging inside and getting angrier as he didn't find what he was looking for.

"Why aren't you at his house?" Marcie said hesitantly.

"Fuck his house!" Simon said.

Marcie glanced at Waylon and continued, "The idea is for you to be there all the time. If you're not—"

"Fuck his house and fuck you," Simon said more emphatically, but his thoughts were still elsewhere. "Know what the miserable little bastard's been doin'? Puttin' new locks on his house. Didn't even think I saw him. Thinks he can put on a crummy lock and feel safe again. I'm gonna show 'im how safe he is."

"At least it shows you've got 'im worried," Marcie said helpfully.

Simon went into his room briefly and emerged again. "Wouldn't have ta worry if he wasn't a goddamned thief." His voice had gone lower, he was talking to himself. "Son of a bitch *owes* me that money. If he don't—"

"Do you know what's occurred to me lately?" Marcie said in a conversational tone. "That maybe he lost your case on purpose. You had a pretty good case but he lost it. And he knew about the money—"

That got Simon's attention. Waylon was looking at her sharply as well.

"Just a thought," she said idly.

Simon stared for a long minute. Marcie started to add something but then kept quiet. Simon finally resumed his search, looking in one last cabinet and then kicking its door closed.

"We got any liquor in this house?" he finally said. Waylon shook his head.

"I'm gonna kill 'im before this is over," Simon said. He stalked back to the still-open front door and started out.

"Now?" Waylon asked.

Simon only slammed the door for response.

The café was a pleasant surprise, a much better than average example of the species. It was lit by small lamps around the walls and on each table, and the dimness probably helped. But Judith and Grey weren't inclined to quibble. The chairs were comfortable, the waitress quick, and the menu more varied than they had expected. There was a bar in the back room, with its own separate entrance and a clientele that held a potential for rowdiness, voices rising above the click of pool cues and balls, but the front room in which they sat was occupied by small family groups. The people at the adjacent tables smiled at Katy, even when she threw her french fries on the floor. Her parents had learned to be grateful for the indulgence of strangers.

"I accept your apology," Grey said.

"For what?"

"You thought this place would be crummy."

"I didn't say that." Judith's answer was low and hurried, because the waitress was returning.

"Sure you did," Grey said, and the waitress said, "How is everything, folks?"

"Just fine." Grey beamed at her. The waitress stepped on one of Katy's french fries and her smile didn't falter. A gem.

"Could I bring you some dessert? Or maybe a drink?"

Judith and Grey looked at each other inquiringly. The waitress adroitly covered the silence: "Most of the big drinking goes on back there, but the elegant crowd out here sometimes likes a nip too." She smiled.

"You have Irish coffee?" Grey asked hesitantly, because such an order in a place like this marked him as an unbearable city slicker.

"You kidding?" the waitress said. "The bartender's name is O'Toole." She made a mark on her pad and seemed pleased.

As if to emphasize her little speech about the back room, there was a sudden swell of noise from that vicinity. Grey twisted around to look, but nothing emerged from the doorway except sound. Two or three voices were raised against one. Grey turned back and shrugged at Judith. "Local color," she said.

A figure rode the next wave of sound out of the back room into theirs. He shook himself angrily, yelled something back into the poolroom, and looked around to see if he was drawing stares. No eyes met his. The waitress blocked Judith's view of him. As soon as she had deposited their cups and started back to the kitchen, Judith gripped Grey's arm and said, "Don't look around."

Grey turned to look at Simon, who still wavered in the doorway. Grey turned back to Judith and said, "Don't worry. Just ignore him."

But Judith's calm was gone. "Did he follow us?" she asked.

"He couldn't have. Probably just wanted a drink. You said yourself this is the only place around."

"Oh damn," Judith said. She looked around for exits, feeling the same helplessness that had trapped her trembling in her bedroom.

"Is he coming this way?"

"Yes."

"Shit," Grey said, and Simon, above him, bellowed, "What did you call me?"

Grey looked up. Simon leaned back from the waist, his mouth open loosely. He swayed a little and his arms swung freely. One hand came close to Grey's ear. "Get away from us,"

Grey said quietly. Katy was looking curiously up at the interloper. Grey felt weighted down by his family.

"What did you say?" Simon shouted again. The two of them were the observed of all observers. Grey pushed his chair back a little and said, "Look." Simon leaned closer to him. One of his hands swung toward Grey's face, and Grey put up a hand to stop it.

*"Ow!"* Simon screamed when the light contact was made. "Trying to kill me?" he shouted, and threw himself on Grey.

Even in that extremity, Grey had too much on his mind. He was aware of Simon on him, bearing him down, of the chair falling back, of one of the glasses on the table tipping. He could see the faces of the nearby diners and imagine the rest of the faces, and he wondered how gracefully he could get out of this, and whether he'd ever come to the café again. All this before the chair and the back of his head hit the floor.

The crack was louder than it was damaging, produced mostly by the chair. But it sounded like a gunshot in the quiet of the café; Grey heard at least one scream. Grey pushed Simon off him and stood. Simon was up first, drawing back a foot to kick Grey in the head if he'd stayed down a moment longer. Grey was groggy and had lost his breath. He held up his hands placatingly, still trying to end the disturbance peacefully. Simon put up his own hands as if he agreed.

"Grey," Judith said. He turned to look at her. She had picked up the baby and stepped back from the table. Grey started to say something calming to her, but during that moment of inattention Simon struck, leaping between Grey's hands and aiming a punch at his face. Grey turned, stepping back, and the blow missed him, but Simon still slammed into him. Simon stank, and his shirt was wet. The contact made Grey feel dirty, as if he'd been in a long fight already, rolling around on the floor. He tried to push Simon away but Simon hit him a glancing blow to the ribs. As Grey doubled over slightly Simon hit him again, a roundhouse right that slammed into Grey's ear. It hurt like hell. It straightened Grey up and maddened him enough to swing furiously at Simon, hitting him in the temple.

Grey's anger quickly faded. As the fight proceeded he realized that he felt, more than anything else, silly. He was reminded of playgrounds. And he had the same problem now he'd had as a boy. He couldn't bring himself to strike as hard as he was able. He pulled his punches, and confined them after that first punch to body blows. He had never been involved in anything like a death struggle, and he couldn't make himself believe that he was in one now. In spite of his grunts and fierce expressions, he was fighting a very restrained battle, mostly trying to protect himself. He also had the problem of having hurt his hand when he'd punched Simon's bony head. He couldn't make a proper fist anymore.

There was another factor operating. Even now, when it seemed the worst was happening, he didn't want to make Simon mad. He feared the man's anger. Even as he fought, he could imagine that Simon was going to take revenge for this occasion. But if no one got hurt it could blow over. Even Simon might feel sheepish about it later, looking back.

Foolishness. Simon roared again and threw himself at Grey. He hurtled between Grey's hands and bore him to the ground. His strong fingers were at Grey's throat. Grey tried to pull him away but his damaged hand couldn't grip. He tried to buck Simon off but the weight was too great this time. Simon was pummeling him with his knees even as he strangled Grey.

Grey could see the faces around him. Startled expressions, open mouths. Many had stood in the first moments but then stopped. Even Judith only looked on in horror, clutching the baby. Grey realized that everyone was frozen except Simon and himself. His breath wouldn't come. It was a terrible shock to realize he was going to be murdered in front of—inches from, in some cases—a dozen eyewitnesses.

# 11

JUDITH POURED HONEY INTO A CUP OF TEA, CAREfully, concentrating on the blending textures. Shifting the spoon to her left hand, she squeezed in lemon juice, threw away the rind, and stirred again. She raised the cup to her mouth, sipped, touched her tongue to her upper lip. Her attention had already left the tea. She stared, seeing nothing, and walked out of the kitchen. The house seemed very empty. Everything had reverted to itself: furniture carried no implications, shadows were only shadows. Simon wasn't outside.

Judith entered the study, listened for a moment, and took the telephone. "Sheriff?" she said. "I'd like to know what you plan to do. Have you heard what—this is Mrs. Stanton—have you heard what happened? Anyone who was there could tell you—What? Yes, all right."

She held the receiver out and said, "He wants to talk to you." Her voice sounded flat even to her, that of a bad actress in a rehearsed conspiracy.

Grey took the phone and resumed his conversation. "Excuse me." He coughed. "Now, what were you saying? I'd already come in to talk to you about this, if you'll remember, and now it seems to be escalating . . . Well, have you talked to anyone?"

"Yes I have," Kendrick said. "I talked to everyone who was there. But the problem is, they don't entirely support your story. Some of the witnesses say you started the fight."

"They said *I* did?"

"Not all of them. But some said you said something to start it, and one said you threw the first punch."

Grey closed his eyes. "You know how unreliable eyewitnesses are," he said. "They never know *what* they've seen."

"That's all I'm saying," the sheriff said sympathetically. "Look, Mr. Stanton, I want to help you. Believe me, I know better than you what Simon Hocksley's like. But you know my problem too, don't you? I can't just go charging in without evidence."

"Sheriff, he almost killed me! Do you hear what my voice sounds like?" Grey looked uneasily at Judith, who was watching him closely.

"Now, I think that's an exaggeration, don't

you, Mr. Stanton? All the witnesses agree that the fight happened very quickly before you were separated and Hocksley left. I know that when you're in the middle of those things they seem to last forever, but that just wasn't the case." Sheriff Kendrick sat at his desk with a patient expression plastered on his face as if Grey could see it. He listened and said, "All I'm telling you is that you won't have a very good case here. He'd have as good a case against you."

"He shouldn't even have been in a place that serves liquor," Grey said. "He's on parole." His eyes sought Judith's. She turned and watched him without expression. Grey sipped his tea and grimaced at the phone. "No, I told you before, I don't want to do that. I just want you to talk to him. If you'd take a hand in this, show him you know what he's doing, I think he'd back off. All right, thank you. I appreciate that." Grey hung up the phone and moved his hand across the cut under his chin, down to his throat.

Sheriff Kendrick looked at the phone and exhaled loudly. Behind his left shoulder, the cell door yawned. The cell hadn't been occupied for more than a year, except when he occasionally went in to sweep it out. Kendrick shuffled his few papers into a pile. His job in this community was a light one: running a speed trap three or four days a month, receiving complaints of noise or trespassing, breaking up an occasional fight. In his five years as sheriff he had never fired his gun. He had taken the job with a slight taste for excitement, but on a day-to-day basis he found himself welcoming dullness. His presence was sufficient to handle almost any trouble that might arise. He didn't look forward to seeing Simon Hocksley.

Kendrick levered himself up from the chair on his thick forearms. He had too much gut, but he was still a powerful man. He was occasionally reminded of that fact, and took pleasure in it. It was an accomplishment of will rather than nature.

James Kendrick's family had moved to the country when he was eight years old. It had been his father's dream to own a small farm. James didn't share the dream, but he didn't say anything. He was a thin, quiet boy, awkward at sports and shy of strangers. In school in Austin he'd managed to find his own niche in a small group of similarly serious-minded boys and girls: good readers, no trouble in class, students the teachers were grateful to call on. Torn from this sanctuary when his parents dislocated him, James was thrown onto his own resources. He found no similar group to cling to in the small country school. Even the good students there were active and boisterous. Everyone seemed bigger than he was, and knowledgeable in areas he'd never heard of. He thought he'd never make friends, the distances between homes making that all the more difficult. He spent all his after-school time at home, usually alone. His sister was a big girl of fourteen, given to long showers and walks in the woods. He secretly followed her one day, having nothing better to do, and watched her stop in a clearing more than a mile from their house. She lay back on the grass, opened her blouse to the sun, and closed her eyes. James watched her lie there for almost an hour, her face unruffled, as if she were taking a recommended therapy. Her little brother was only vaguely interested himself, but he stored the information as something that might prove useful.

Meanwhile, his problems at school worsened. From a novelty he had become an object of ridicule. He was being tested, but he took it only for torment, and allowed himself to be driven away. He kept apart from most of the children, but there were a few who wouldn't let him withdraw completely. Chief among these were the Hocksley brothers. Waylon was his age, and Simon was in their class as well, though he was older, a tall boy with an already old contempt for teachers and good students. Waylon was his accomplice. Waylon would kneel behind you while Simon pushed you over. A week never passed in which they didn't trap him into a fight or a humiliation. The grown Kendrick remembered those fights vividly: Waylon whooping and capering and stooping to tweak his nose while James and Simon struggled in the dust until Simon had him pinned, sitting on his stomach and stapling his wrists to the ground with his hands. Once he had him like that he would slide forward, and James couldn't dislodge him no matter how much he bucked and struggled. Simon would inch forward until he could put his knees on James's arms. Then he would sit back and grin, enjoying the smaller boy's pain and embarrassment, until he decided what new pain to inflict. The one James hated worst was when Simon leaned forward to pinch the insides of his upper arms. With his arms pinned and drawn taut by Simon's legs, the pain was intense. The feeling of helplessness was worse. He would howl then, not caring that that was what Simon wanted, until a teacher came to stop it or Simon grew bored with the game.

This went on for an eternity—a few weeks—until he realized he could never beat the brothers, and he tried to make friends with them instead. "Do you want to see something?" he asked the next time they trapped him in a corner of the playground. The Hocksleys grinned and elbowed each other and finally let themselves be bought off. After school James took them home with him and the three of them hid near the house with cookies James had brought to distract them. They stayed there, Simon occasionally pinching James or twisting his arm in spite of the truce, until James saw his sister emerge from the back door and saunter toward the woods. He put his fingers to his lips and the three of them crept after her. Simon and Waylon were less quiet than James, so that he had to keep waving them back, but Joan never seemed to notice. She picked her way through the woods to her usual sunny clearing and, while the boys watched, removed her blouse and bra. Her breasts were nearly as brown as her face. James watched Simon for a reaction. Simon stared and chortled, until James was sure Joan would hear them, and Waylon clamped a hand over his brother's mouth. The two of them stood goggling and punching each other. They ignored James when he plucked at their sleeves, and he finally wandered away alone and uninjured.

The bribery was not a success. The next day in school Simon and Waylon had a rhyme which was soon making its way through their little gang, and with it a new nickname for James. He knew the first time he heard someone singing "Titty Baby" behind his back that it referred to him and that the story was known to everyone.

Kendrick still cringed when he thought of

that childish name. He had outlived the incident and had managed to make some friends by the time that first school year was over. Simon and Waylon moved on to other victims. James got his normal growth spurts in a few years; in high school he played football and lifted weights and had come to enjoy country life as much as his father. He no longer thought about moving back to Austin. Simon and Waylon had left school by that time, which Kendrick regretted, because it meant they would remember him, if at all, as nothing more than a crying eight-year-old child. When he thought of Simon he felt the ghost twinges of those old pains inside his upper arms. There was a deep-rooted hatred in Kendrick, but it was coupled with the discipline he'd imposed on himself for years. He would have loved the opportunity to prove to Simon that he had made himself into a man Simon should fear physically, but his image of himself and his job was more important. He wouldn't abuse his authority to settle a childhood grudge.

Isolated as they were, they could always hear a car coming well before they saw it. Simon, at the window, grunted and said, "Waylon."

Waylon looked up from his corner, from the wheelchair.

"Sheriff," Simon said.

Waylon nodded glumly. Simon didn't see him move, but he knew he had heard.

Simon jerked the door open as soon as the first knock fell. Kendrick stood with his fist raised, and awkwardly lowered it. "Sheriff!" Simon said loudly, all grins. "What on earth brings you all the way out here?"

"Like to talk to you," Kendrick said.

"Surely, surely. What've you got to say?"

Kendrick shifted his feet, waiting for an invitation that didn't come. Simon leaned on the open door and smiled lazily. Kendrick said deeply, "Hear you got into a little trouble last night."

"Ah, shoot, I've done lots worse'n that without gittin' the law on me." Simon affected surprise. His grin denied the reality of their talk, urged Kendrick to say what he'd really come for.

The sheriff's face remained impassive. "Well, I don't know about that. I do know you got in a fight at the café. You mind if I come in? Little warm out here."

"Why sure, sure. What'm I doin'? Get on in here."

Simon flung his arm out in invitation, but didn't step back. Kendrick waited a moment, then squeezed through the narrow opening, his face passing inches from Simon's. Inside, the room was dim and cluttered. Kendrick gave it a quick glance and returned his attention to Simon.

"Put on a little weight, haven't you, sheriff. Looks good, looks good. I remember when you were such a skinny little thing."

"All right, I don't want to take too long with this, Simon. I've had a complaint from the man you attacked in the café."

"*Me* attack? Why, sheriff, you shoulda seen the way that man jumped on me. First called me a name I wouldn't repeat, then grabbed my arm and practically broke it."

"You're on parole, Simon. You should never—"

"That doesn't mean I cain't defend myself, does it, sheriff? What would be the point of them lettin' me out of the jug if they gonna let me git killed by the first runty little tourist that wants to, and they say I'm just supposed to stand there and take it? You cain't expect a man to live like that, sheriff. If it's the law, okay, slap the cuffs on me right now, but it sure ain't fair."

The sheriff hooked his thumbs in his belt and stood wearily through this. He ignored Simon's outstretched hands, ready for the handcuffs. "You know that's not what I'm saying, Simon. Of course you can defend yourself—"

"Well, good."

"But that's not the way I heard it from some of the witnesses. Some of them say you attacked *him.* And what's more, Mr. Stanton tells me this isn't the first run-in you've had."

"Now, that's just not true, sheriff. I hadn't laid a hand on him before he dropped on me like a ton of earthworms. If you're gonna take me in for that—"

"Nobody's said anything about taking you in," Kendrick said. There were faint noises from the next room. Kendrick glanced that way, but the door was closed. He shifted his weight from one leg to the other. He and Simon still stood. No one had offered him a seat, and Kendrick wasn't sure he would have wanted to sit on any of the furniture. The chair behind him looked rickety enough to collapse under the weight of its dust.

"You mean you're not arrestin' me, sheriff?" Simon looked pitifully grateful, but he still wore that grin that denied everything.

"No. But I want to give you a warning."

Now a voice drifted out of the next room, thin, piping, delivering a singsong chant. Kendrick flushed red at the first syllables, but went on talking, ignoring the childish sound.

*"Went to the country, had to leave the city . . ."*

"Stanton has told me what's going on, how you're harassing him. I just want you to know that I've heard about it, so if something happens to him I'll know right where to come look."

*". . . 'Cause he went and peeked at his sister's titty."*

Simon's grin had grown wider. He nodded slightly, asking Kendrick to acknowledge what they were hearing. Clearly he wasn't listening to the warning, but Kendrick went doggedly on while the voice from the next room repeated the rhyme.

"You hear me, Simon? I don't know what kind of grudge you think you've got against Stanton, but whatever it is, you come to me with it. I don't want you trespassing on his property or threatening him. You've got no right, whatever you think he's done."

More noises from the next room. Footsteps on creaking boards. The voice was a little louder. It had gone into the chorus: "Titty Baby, Titty Baby," repeated over and over to a mindless tune. Kendrick's hands opened and closed.

The bedroom door opened and Waylon came in saying the old nickname one last time. He stopped at the picture before him. "Why, looka here. I didn't know you was here, sheriff." He came forward with a grin to match Simon's, but more diffident, shy. It was hard to connect his innocent face with the chant, but Kendrick had seen that expression too many times.

"Yeah, look at him," Simon said proudly. "All growed up. And growed out. Look at this muscle."

He squeezed a bit of the extra flesh at the sheriff's waist, showing it to Waylon. Kendrick jerked away.

"Don't do that again!" His hand moved involuntarily to his gun.

"Why, I'm sorry, sheriff. I was just showin' my brother what a fine big man you was. Don't shoot me."

Kendrick moved his hand away from the gun. "Don't be ridiculous."

"Wow, and carries a gun, too," Waylon said behind him. "Just like a cowboy." He made a whizzing sound and Kendrick felt a tug at his hip. "Bang!" Waylon said loudly.

Kendrick grabbed at his gun and found it still in its holster. Waylon, still standing behind him, grinned at him again.

"Now, look," Kendrick said loudly. "Both of you back off. I'm not here to pick a fight with you. This is just a warning for you, Simon, it's got nothing to do with Waylon."

"Who's trying to pick a fight?" Simon said wonderingly. He looked over Kendrick's shoulder and said, "Are you, Waylon? Waylon?" His eyes traveled downward.

Kendrick quickly looked over his shoulder and saw only the door. He looked down and saw Waylon bending over behind him. At that moment he felt Simon's hand on his chest and he started to go over backward. His arms flailed.

Simon caught one of them and steadied him. He kept his hands on the sheriff's shoulder and looked at him with concern.

"Are you all right, sheriff? Careful you don't fall over him. What're you doin' down there, Waylon, you idiot?"

Waylon straightened up and offered the bullet he'd picked up from the floor. "Here, sheriff, did you drop this? I just saw it lyin' there, and I figured you wouldn't want to lose it."

It was the playground all over again. They both stared at him with sympathetic expressions that slipped on the smiles underneath. They acted as if they'd never grown up. Kendrick was seething. When he'd felt himself starting to fall backward he had been ready to kill them both. Now he pictured the subsequent trial: "And what did these men do to you to make you shoot them each six times in the face, Sheriff Kendrick?" "They pinched me. They pretended to grab my gun, and acted like they were going to push me onto my back. Twenty years ago they made up a nickname for me." "And what was the nickname, sheriff?" Everyone laughing, from the jury box to the back doors of the courtroom.

"Look," Kendrick said fiercely. "Get around here." He grabbed Waylon and pulled him around to stand beside his brother. "I didn't come here to play games with you two." Their eyes widened; whatever was he talking about?

"Now, make sure you're listening this time. I want you to leave Stanton alone. Whatever you've been doing to him, stop it. This is the only warning you're getting."

Simon said, "You mean don't walk past his house, sheriff? 'Cause that's th' only thing I've done. Are you telling me to stay off the public road?"

"You know what I'm telling you. Lay off!"

Kendrick gave them a glare that had no effect on their expressions, then spun on his heel and launched himself out the door. Behind its slamming he heard the brothers breaking into the laughter they'd been suppressing. Kendrick was almost blind with rage. Nothing would have given him more pleasure than beating them both to death, or shooting them where they stood. And his chance might come. But he wouldn't do it without an excellent cause. Today they'd won by reverting to the tactics of the schoolyard. They wouldn't acknowledge that years had passed, that their positions had changed. Kendrick would eventually change that, he told himself, by sticking to the absolute letter of the law. Formal complaint or no formal complaint. He banged his fender on a sapling as he spun out of the dirt yard. Inside the cloud of dust he ground his teeth, and not all his anger was directed at the brothers Hocksley.

* * *

The next night, Grey and Judith returned from Austin in high spirits. They were both slightly drunk after an evening spent in restaurants and bars with old friends. They had danced. They had sat at opposite ends of a table and felt as if they were holding hands. Everyone had remarked that country life seemed to agree with them. The surprise in their friends' voices had made the Stantons smile.

They hadn't seen Simon for two days.

The sheriff's visit to Hocksley appeared to have been effective. There'd been no sign of him since; it seemed certain he'd given up his ridiculous quest. There was a Simon-sized hole in the landscape across the road from their house, but it was gradually filling in. In a few days he would no longer even be conspicuous by his absence. Their house and their lives belonged to them again, and they realized with happy surprise what a short ordeal it had really been. One should learn not to overreact to these things. As they drove through the night the surrounding hills, which had been closing like a fist with them in the palm, opened up again, leaving them in a secure valley.

Katy lay sleeping in Judith's arms. She'd awakened briefly when they'd picked her up from Judith's parents' house, but had dropped off again immediately.

"You know what I think?" Grey said. "I think I may give up this book idea and go back to work." He saw he had her curiosity. "I know, my lifelong dream. But I've realized since I took time off that if I really want to write it I could have done it in my spare time. Now I feel too pressured. Just staring at the paper. Now that I have to do it, it's no fun."

"Well, um . . ." Judith looked out her window.

"Are you smirking?"

"No. I'm not, no."

"Yes you are. You're practically laughing out loud."

She did, then, allow a small escape of laughter.

"You thought this would happen, didn't you?" Grey accused. When she chuckled again his rueful look deepened, but it could be seen that he was hiding a small store of amusement himself.

"No, I didn't know. I thought there was a chance, though."

"You're such a smart woman." He let some of the laughter into his voice.

Judith reached for his arm and slid her hand along it. He dropped it from the steering wheel and their hands held. The car pulled them through the night, darkness parting briefly for their headlights.

"So what will you do?" Judith asked. "Go back to the office?"

"I suppose. Harry will be glad to see me. He

won't ask me to come back, but you can see that my staying away is driving him crazy. He needs a good-guy partner to make him look shifty." Pause. "He'll consider it a personal triumph when I tell him I'm quitting the book."

"He'll see that it bothers you. I don't think he'll rub it in."

Grey looked at her askance, and another silence fell. Their exuberance had diffused and softened into a comfortable mood that covered them like bedclothes. They were alone on the road. Katy breathed easily on Judith's lap. She stirred slightly and they both looked at her as if she'd introduced a new topic.

"Will you start back right away?"

"No. I'll call Harry in the morning, but I'll wait a few days to go back." He hesitated to say why, but Judith knew, of course.

"We'll be all right."

He didn't answer. She squeezed his hand. "He won't be coming back, Grey. It was a silly idea and he must have given up on it by now. The sheriff probably had a talk with him and straightened everything out."

He shrugged.

"Besides, I'll be gone a lot of the time myself. I'll be spending more time in Austin and Katy will be at my mother's. I'll even leave her with you if that will make you feel easier."

"Thanks."

"He can't do anything if we're not there. And

don't forget those wonderful locks you installed. You go off every day leaving us behind those and we'll be safe as in a castle. With a moat."

Grey smiled. They were close to their darkened house.

"It's funny to be talking about going back so soon. I wanted this time off for so long."

"And worked so hard for it," she credited him.

"Mmm. At one time I would have done anything for it."

She squeezed his hand again, drawing him out of his abstraction. He looked at her and slowly matched her smile. They rode in silence until they pulled into their driveway. Katy moaned softly when Judith raised her to her shoulder, and Grey hurried around the car in case they needed help. They stood under the porch light and Judith crooned to the baby while he inserted his key and pushed. He bumped his knuckles against the door when it held closed. He and Judith looked at each other, puzzled, until he smiled, remembering, and sorted through his key chain for the other key, the one that fit the new lock. He displayed it to Judith before using it. The new lock was a little stiff, he might have to oil it. It was possible, too, that the key didn't fit perfectly. The lock resisted it for a moment, he had to jiggle the key. But he liked to feel the weight of the mechanism. Judith, behind him, was glancing across the road nervously.

She swept past him toward the living room as soon as the door opened. Grey stood in the hall relocking it. For a moment the thin light in the hall had to serve for the whole house.

"It's just as well I got these locks," Grey was telling her loudly as he turned the tumblers and tested the knob. "We should have replaced the old ones anyway, and these are much better."

"As long as we don't get killed on the porch," Judith said as she turned into the living room, "while we're trying to get into our—" Her voice stopped abruptly.

Grey turned into the living room and almost bumped into her back. Her breath was indrawn so quickly it was a shriek in reverse. Grey reached past her to turn on the light.

Judith sighed. "Oh God, I thought there was someone crouching on the floor in front of me. It's just this chair out of place."

She reached to push it back, still holding Katy, and turned to Grey, expecting his help. But he was stopped as abruptly as she had been, staring beyond her. When she looked past the chair in front of her she saw that her attention had been too restricted. Grey walked stiffly past her to the sofa, whose cushions were jumbled atop each other. He tried absent-mindedly to push them into place, then lifted one and dropped it to the floor. Bare springs showed through the slashed upholstery.

The bookcase was empty, most of the books on the floor hidden behind the sofa. While Judith stared Grey walked around it and picked up a book at random. Its spine was broken. When he held it up a few pages lost their hold and fluttered to the floor to join the pile there.

Only the overhead light had come on. The floor lamp was on its side and bent. When Grey walked past it his steps crackled as if he walked on bird bones. He righted the lamp but it wobbled and fell again with a crash that startled Katy into silent wakefulness. Unconsciously rocking her, Judith walked past the broken sofa toward the hallway to the kitchen.

"Wait," Grey said. He looked around for a weapon, saw nothing, and came past her. His face was blank. Judith's still registered only puzzlement. She watched him slip cautiously through the doorway ahead of her, then she followed quickly.

The chief victim in the kitchen appeared to be a set of plates. Their fragments covered the floor in a spatter pattern, as if the whole set had been tossed in a pack toward the ceiling. Small slides of clearing showed that someone had walked through the mess, but there was no clear footprint. All the cabinet doors were open, and fragments of other dishes were mixed with those of the plates. A whole coffee cup lay on the dust, its fall apparently cushioned by its fallen mates.

Grey carefully circled the area of greatest destruction, peeked around the refrigerator, and tried the back door. It was locked. He came back, glancing into the cabinets and opening the one closed door in the room. No one was hiding in the pantry. As an afterthought he picked up the phone, listened, and held it toward Judith. She heard the unbroken drone of the dial tone.

The storm had begun in Grey's study, and it had absorbed the brunt of the damage. Papers carpeted the floor almost without interruption. Some of them crunched because there was broken glass underneath. The window had been shattered and then raised, providing access to the house.

The typewriter lay on its keys on the floor, one ribbon spool unwound from its mooring to the far corner of the room. Two or three footsteps on it had ground its ink into the papers underneath. One of the prints seemed to be that of a dog.

The drawers had been pulled from the desk and most lay bottom-up. One of them had been splintered against the desk itself. Books were scattered in this room as well, some of them slumped against the wall opposite the bookcase, flung with great energy. A framed print had slid straight down the wall from its hook.

Two long cracks in its glass met and formed an arrow that pointed at Judith's face as she stood in the doorway. She still showed no fear, and Katy made no sound. Both of them stared at Grey where he stood in the middle of the damage with his back to them. When he turned he gave them a wan smile before brushing past them.

Judith followed him to the staircase. He started up it slowly, then turned back to put a warning finger to his lips and wave her cautiously up behind him. "Call the sheriff," he whispered, and pointed back to the kitchen. Judith looked toward it but didn't move, reluctant to leave him. But when she turned back he was already moving up into the darkness. She hurried to the kitchen and dialed the number Grey had written on a pad beside the phone. The ringing went on but no one answered. Judith would have to find the sheriff's home number. Instead, she glanced through the doorway, then dropped the phone on its hook and hurried upstairs to be with Grey.

Lights were on now. She rushed into the bedroom and stopped, relieved to see Grey standing there. The intruder's energy had begun to dwindle by the time he'd gotten this far. Most of the clothes had been flung out of the closet, but none seemed otherwise damaged. The mattress had been pulled off the box spring, but only the former had been slashed, and that only superficially. Grey looked at her and shrugged. "Check the bathroom," she said quietly.

"I did," he said, but Judith walked past him and looked in herself. The shower curtain was pulled down, the stall empty. The mirror was cracked and the medicine cabinet open. Only one shelf had been emptied of its contents, those scattered on the floor and in the sink.

Judith turned to see that Grey had left the room, and she hurried after him. He was in the game room. The new lock still held the door here as well, but a couple of its glass panes had been shattered, probably by billiard balls. The others rolled underfoot. The top of the table was empty; there was one long slash down the middle of its felt.

Grey's face had gone blank again. Judith was more worried about him than about the house. "The nursery?" she said, mostly to break the stillness. Grey shrugged. The light burned at the end of the hall, so he had already checked the baby's room. The housebreaker had fled.

Judith followed him downstairs and reported the lack of results of her phone call. Grey took the time to look up the sheriff's home number. He watched her as he dialed, and smiled and reached a playful finger toward Katy while he waited for an answer. Judith took an easier breath than she had since entering the house. One good thing about the wreckage of the house was that it couldn't possibly be her imagination. The siege had escalated into an official matter, something for the sheriff to handle.

"Hello," Grey said. "Sheriff? Did I wake you?"

"What? No, no."

Grey sensed the untruth of that and wondered fleetingly why no one likes to admit to having been asleep. But he hurried on, keeping his voice low for the benefit of his wife and daughter. "This is Grey Stanton. My wife and I have just returned from an evening in Austin, and our house has been broken into. . . . No, we haven't found anything missing and I don't think we will. It was Hocksley."

"What?" Grey heard Kendrick stir, and animation enter the sheriff's voice for the first time. "You saw him? You didn't catch him, did you?"

"No—"

"But you saw him? You know it was him."

"Of course it was Hocksley," Grey said. "It's just another step in his harassment. Did you ever go talk to him?"

Kendrick was one of those people who seem instantly alert when awakened but don't actually start thinking for several minutes. Now he remembered his visit to Simon and anger thawed his mind.

"I talked to him, all right. I told him just what would happen if he kept it up."

"Well, he has," Grey said calmly. "You'll just have to pick him up this time. Now I *will* swear out a complaint."

There was a brief silence as Kendrick almost snapped at him. If he'd had a complaint the first time, he wouldn't have made such a fool of himself. Now . . . But he controlled his voice when he answered. "Burglary isn't just a question of a complaint, Mr. Stanton, I'm sure you know. If all it took to put someone in jail was a complaint, the jails'd be full."

"They are full," Grey said.

"Fuller, then. You know what I mean. I have to have evidence. Did the burglar leave anything behind, something identifiable, blood, or—"

Grey noted the fact that the sheriff said "the burglar" rather than "Simon," leaving it in the realm of theory. "I haven't checked for fingerprints," he said thickly, "but I strongly doubt he left any."

"They never seem to, do they?" the sheriff said.

Grey was getting mad. "It would be great for your case if he killed me, wouldn't it?" he said before he remembered Judith and Katy were in the room. Judith looked at him with alarm.

Only if someone saw him do it, the sheriff thought, but kept silent. Grey exhaled. He had been on the other side of this argument many times as a defense lawyer, and knew Kendrick was right. It was obvious Simon was behind this, but obviousness isn't proof.

"I'll come out and see what I can find," Kendrick said.

"You might as well wait until morning," Grey told him. "We're very tired."

He was, suddenly. He tried to think of what he should do but couldn't. Calling the sheriff had been a last resort itself.

Judith was startled to see him hang up the phone. Grey's weariness frightened her. "He's not going to do anything," she said, hoping to be contradicted. "What's the matter?" She became suddenly aware of the large black kitchen window and stepped around the refrigerator out of its sight.

"Well," Grey said. "We seem to be on our own."

# 12

WHEN THE BED SHIFTED IN THE MORNING JUdith woke, as she had often during the night. She lay with eyes closed, trying to hang on to the protection of sleep. The night had been a tiring mix of watchful waking and watchful sleep: even when she'd slept she'd dreamed she was awake, lying in the bed listening for any sound, watching for any movement. As a result she wasn't sure now that she was awake, wasn't sure that everything hadn't been a dream.

She opened her eyes and looked at the ceiling. It was the largest expanse in the room that would show no effects of the damage, so by keeping her eyes on it she could sustain the illusion of normality. But she was wide enough awake now to know that her memory was real. Katy was curled against her right side. She and Grey had spent the night with the baby between them, after Grey had dragged the mattress back aboard its box spring. With a new sheet it had been perfectly usable, though Judith could feel beneath her how the foam stuffing had shifted, pressing toward the escape of the slashes in the middle.

Beyond Katy the bed was empty. She'd been awakened by Grey's rising. His night must have been as bad as hers. Every time she'd come awake during the night she'd felt his wakefulness, but they hadn't spoken or touched across Katy. Grey had stayed in the same position, rigidly on his back. Judith imagined his eyes open all night.

Katy stirred and opened her eyes. "Hello," Judith said cheerfully, but Katy couldn't be humored on first awakening. She opened and closed her eyes slowly and soon began squirming.

Grey was in the bathroom. When he came out his face wore the same expression—none—he'd had all last night. To Judith it seemed that his mind, busy with something vital, had given up the relatively unimportant job of manipulating his face. At the dresser he doffed his pajamas and dressed quickly, his back to her. He didn't even sit to put on his shoes—boots today—just bent and pulled them on in one motion, as if his feet had gone boneless. Everything cooperated not to disturb the tension in him.

He went out without a word. Judith rose quickly to find a robe and slippers. Katy was watching her alertly, so she picked her up and took her along, stopping in the nursery for a bag of diapers.

Grey was on the sofa in the living room. She almost walked past him, expecting to find him in the kitchen. She deposited Katy beside him and began changing her.

"Good morning."

"You'd better get dressed," he said. "The sheriff ought to be here soon." When Judith gestured at Katy he said, "I'll do that," so she left him to it and went upstairs to dress.

She started toward the kitchen when she came down, but he stopped her.

"Better leave it alone, I think. Don't clean anything up until he's seen it all."

"Can I make coffee?"

After consideration, Grey thought that would be all right. They sat on the sofa with their coffee cups and Katy between them, a mirror image of their night's positions. Katy wanted to play in the debris, and grew cranky when they stopped her.

"I'm going out there," Grey said abruptly. "As soon as the sheriff's been here I'm going to go out and talk to Hocksley. It's time to put a stop to this."

"What about the sheriff?"

"I don't think he's going to do anything."

"Why?"

"Can't. Where's his evidence?"

"I'm going with you," she said after a moment.

"And Katy?" His voice was almost pleasant, anticipatory, not the toneless thing she expected to come from him. She frowned at the mention of the baby. Grey saw he had made his point. "No, here's what I want you to do. As soon as the sheriff leaves I want you to go into town and see Harry. Tell him to contact the parole office, find out who Simon's officer is, and let him know what's been going on. Tell him everything—being in a bar, the fight. Tell him the sheriff's warned him once. If they decide that's enough to revoke, tell them we'll cooperate. Sign something if Harry checks it first. After you do that, if Harry's not satisfied and wants to go to a judge on his own, that's fine too."

"And what are you going to be doing?"

"Seeing if I can stop it without all that."

After that they sat in silence until the sheriff came. Grey met him at the door and gave him a tour of the destruction. Kendrick had a fingerprint kit and seemed to know how to use it, but he found nothing helpful. Judith saw by the end of the investigation that the two men had grown stiff and polite with each other. Events seemed to have devolved into some male ritual she didn't understand or approve of. The sheriff had been sympathetic when he arrived, but Grey's coolness had put him off. They both knew the sheriff wouldn't find anything useful. He left promising to investigate further, and Grey closed the door behind him as if an unpleasant duty were over.

"Got your purse?" he said at once. Judith went for it and carried Katy to the car. Grey watched them pull out and waited until they were out of sight before he got into his own car and left in the opposite direction.

Lucinda Carmack had described to him where Simon lived. His resolve diminished slightly as he neared the house, but he had been hoarding anger all night and it didn't fail him now. Turning off the road onto the dirt track, he felt he passed a barrier, leaving law and his protection behind. Trees pressed close, quickly cutting off any sight but the ruts immediately ahead.

He could not have explained clearly what he was doing. A great unreasoning calm had taken him at the first sight of the destruction in his house. He was suddenly immersed in Simon's world. Law became a dim idea, less substantial than an odor. Grey had made his concession to the law this morning, but he was compelled toward a confrontation. He wanted to see Simon face to face to demand an explanation and an ending.

The trees broke apart and admitted him suddenly to the clearing occupied by the ramshackle house. Seeing it, Grey could believe what Lucinda had told him about Simon's income. He stepped out onto soft ground barren of grass. Chickens watched him distrustfully behind their fence. Grey closed his door softly, but it was the loudest sound for miles.

Now he wished himself gone. But he felt watched. He wouldn't get back in his car and leave now that he had come. He lengthened his stride. Drawing close to the door took him out of range of the windows.

He knocked lightly. The ripples of the knock spread through the whole loose structure of the house, but no sound answered. He wouldn't have been surprised by a gun blast. Silence did surprise him. He raised his hand to knock again, but instead opened his fingers and pushed. The door, not firmly closed, opened a foot and drifted toward him again. Grey pushed through it and looked inside.

This was where shadows hid from the sun. The room held more than its share of darkness, considering the bright day Grey had stepped in from. Dust frosted the windows, and there were no interior lights. The situation seemed suited to the furniture, which might not have survived direct sunlight.

It took some seconds for Grey to see the one figure in the room. He stepped back quickly toward the door, and opened his mouth to explain. But the man wasn't moving, and when he looked closer Grey saw that it was a wheelchair in which the man sat slumped.

Grey moved silently closer. A rifle, the same .22 Simon had carried, leaned against the wheelchair, its barrel pointed past the crown of the man's head. When Grey got close enough he snatched the gun away. The figure stirred and raised his head, blinking. As a sentry, if that was his job, he wasn't much use.

"Wha'?" he said. "Who're you?"

Grey told him his name. "You must be Waylon." No one had told him the brother was crippled. Maybe it had been a recent accident. Waylon was glancing fearfully from Grey's face to the rifle. To reassure him, Grey looked around and found two sets of antlers close together on the wall. He raised the rifle above his head, out of the cripple's reach, and set it on the antlers. They might have been placed there for that purpose.

"I just came to see Simon."

"Not here," Waylon said, watching him anxiously. He lowered his hands to the wheels and pushed the chair back a few inches, then forward the same distance. "What are you gonna do?"

"Wait," Grey said shortly. "You expect him back soon?"

Waylon only stared at him with wide eyes and slightly lowered head. Grey moved to a door on his right and opened it to reveal a small bedroom. A glance under the bed and into the closet showed no one was hiding there. He slammed the closet door a little too sharply and the whole room seemed to shiver. When Grey turned, Waylon was in the doorway watching him. When Grey advanced toward the door, Waylon rolled quickly backward and put an arm up to his face, so that the wheelchair slewed to the side.

"Don't hurt me," he whimpered.

Grey looked at him coldly. He had lost his own uneasiness in the face of this fear. He walked toward Waylon, who backed away again, head still down. Grey stopped and bent toward him. "I'd just like you to tell me something. Do you know what's been going on between your brother and me? What he's been doing to my family and me?"

"I don't have nothin' to do with any of that," Waylon said loudly, almost with a challenge under the whine.

"I didn't think you did. I just thought you might be able to help me, give me some idea why Simon fixed on me as the one who robbed him."

Waylon just stared and shook his head violently. Grey sighed quietly and straightened up. "What's back there?" he asked, pointing across the room to another closed door.

"Nothing, sir. Just the kitchen and my room."

"Mind if I look?" Grey's tone made it clear he wasn't waiting for permission. He started across the room. He heard the wheels and glanced back to see that Waylon had moved under the antlers. The rifle was four feet above his head. Grey continued toward the doorway. He heard a slight straining of fabric as Waylon apparently bounced in the chair in an effort to reach the rifle, but it was well out of his reach. Grey didn't worry until he heard the voice close behind him. "Yeah—" Waylon said in a new tone, and Grey turned to see him on his feet behind him, with the gun pointed at Grey's navel. "I mind."

The wheelchair still sat under the antlers. Waylon's pitifulness had been left in it. He stared levelly at Grey, his hatred more menacing than the gun. Grey, who had jumped back at first sight of him standing, raised his open hands to waist level and shuffled to the side. Waylon let him edge around in a half-circle until his back was toward the front door, then advanced. Grey stood his ground until the gun barrel was embedded in his stomach.

"What do you want here?" Waylon said.

"I told you, just to talk to Simon. Be careful." The gun barrel was terribly hard. It seemed to be intruding inside him, making his stomach churn and his breath come in short gasps.

Waylon said speculatively, "I bet one of these

little bitty bullets wouldn't kill you even at this range."

"It's got nothing to do with you." Grey spoke very fast. He moved one very tentative hand toward the rifle but jerked it back when Waylon pressed harder. Grey felt his upraised hands growing cold as they lost blood circulation. "I'll try to talk to Simon some other time," he said quickly. "Just let me . . . Take it easy."

Waylon pulled the trigger. "Bang!" he shouted, but the only other sound was the click of the hammer falling on the empty chamber. Grey leaped backward before he realized he hadn't been shot. Waylon threw the rifle aside and sprang toward him. They were moving in the same direction. Waylon's weight slammed Grey back against the door and Waylon held him there by a forearm at his throat. Waylon's voice sank.

"You don't come around here again. And if I'as you I'd be careful about accusin' my brother of anything. He's had some bad experience along those lines."

Grey pushed him away, hard. Waylon skidded back a couple of steps and stopped, glaring. Grey had gone suddenly stiff. His voice came out very tight, that of a man controlling some powerful emotion, but Grey himself could not have said which one. His hoarse breathing could have been taken for fear or anger. "Tell

Simon this," he said in a voice loud enough to carry across the room. "I've already started steps to have his parole revoked. If he comes near my house again, it'll be the last place he goes outside of prison for the next several years."

Waylon didn't respond in any way. Grey went quickly out the door.

A minute after they heard the sound of his car diminishing, Simon and Marcie came out of the doorway behind Waylon.

"Now, what's got him so stirred up?" Simon asked with more wonder than anger.

"You're getting to him," Marcie said. She stroked his arm. "He's ready to crack."

"Must be. Waylon, what'd you say to him when you were talkin' so low?"

Waylon finally turned. He didn't meet Marcie's eyes, which were on him. "Nothin'. Told him not to come around no more."

Simon nodded. "I'm gonna have to kill him now," he said. Now the anger started to appear. "He thinks he's gonna send me back. I won't let 'im do that."

"That's right," Marcie said.

Her encouragement seemed to deflate Simon. He looked thoughtful. "You know, I had just started to think I might've been wrong about him, that maybe he don't have my money."

"Of course he took it," Marcie said. She

looked at Waylon for support but he didn't say anything. "What's the matter, you scared of him all of a sudden?"

"'Course not," Simon said, but his anger wasn't rekindled.

"All right, look," Marcie said with an edge of contempt. *"I'll* find out, okay? Just so we're all sure."

"How?" Waylon said.

"Don't worry, he'll tell me the truth."

Simon shrugged. "I don't care. Do what ya want. . . . And then I'll do what I want," he added.

Grey sat in the living room with a drink beside him. The deadbolt lock on the front door hadn't been relocked. He couldn't believe that this already-broken-into house was subject to any more immediate attacks. He stared at the empty bookshelves. As soon as he had the energy he'd rise and start putting them back in order. He was in no hurry. The evidence of the first violation made him feel safe from another.

He was tired. He hadn't slept all night. The anger that had carried him out the door of Waylon's house had left him feeling very drained when it faded away. But everything would be over soon. Simon would leave them alone or would go back to jail. It was a matter of law again. He didn't even stand up when the front door opened.

"Hello?" A woman's voice. Grey relaxed further. Not Judith, but familiar. "Helloooo." Footsteps brought the voice into the room where he sat facing the doorway. He didn't acknowledge her, but picked up his drink and sipped again.

"My goodness," Marcie said. "Is it all like this?" He looked at her without offering a greeting. "Sorry for barging in," she went on carelessly, "but it was open and I thought you wouldn't mind company. What happened here?"

"Don't you know?" Grey said. Marcie looked at him suspiciously, but he only meant he thought the news would be widespread by now. He wasn't surprised to see Marcie. His was quite literally an open house. Soon they'd all be trooping in: Harry, Fran, Kendrick, Lucinda Carmack, Simon. . . .

Marcie left him, to look through the rest of the downstairs. He heard her footsteps crunch. "God!" she called from the kitchen. "This looks terrible."

There didn't seem to be an answer to that, so he just waited for her to reappear. When she did she appeared to notice for the first time how quiet he was. She bent to peer at him. He looked back levelly. Marcie's expression was sympathetic, but her eyes were almost merry. "Simon Hocksley?" she asked.

"We assume."

She came even closer. Her bright eyes were in vivid contrast to his. "What are you going to do about it?" she asked.

"I'm not sure yet. Maybe try to get his parole revoked."

"Better not let him hear about that." She continued to study him. Her expression grew happier. "Are you starting to think it wasn't worth it?" she asked quietly.

"What wasn't?"

"Taking his money."

He looked at her more closely. Now he realized that the laughter in her eyes was a conspiratorial look. "You've got it, don't you?" she said.

"Of course not."

"You can tell me." She leaned even closer. Grey turned slightly away. Her lips were very close to his ear when she said, "I know you took it."

"Don't be crazy," he said harshly.

"I can help you." Her voice deepened, lost its playfulness. "Split it with me. I've seen Simon. He'll believe me if I tell him you don't have it."

Grey drew back and looked at her sharply. She nodded.

She met Simon back at the house in the woods. She strode in without knocking, wearing the same triumphant expression she'd given Grey. Simon looked up from the floor where he leaned against the wall, the rifle disassembled in his hands. He didn't speak, but his expression asked a question.

"He's got it all right," Marcie said. "He told me." She laughed.

# 13

THE HOUSE IS CLEAN AGAIN, AND SOON IT WILL be quiet. At the moment it is full of the last-minute sounds of Grey and Judith getting ready to go out. Their noise populates the house, making it safe. Grey is in his study shuffling papers. Judith, from upstairs, calls to him, and he steps to the doorway to answer. He can hear her steps tapping quickly back and forth overhead.

They are bound in opposite directions. Harry, learning that Grey is working for the firm again, has asked him to locate a witness in the next county west. Judith is going to Mr. Rhodes's new office in Austin, where she is to meet the men delivering his new furniture. Upstairs, she glances at her reflection. She looks pale, her lipstick stands out in the mirror. Today is the first time she will see the actual furniture actually in the office. Today it will be apparent to her, and more important, to Mr. Rhodes, whether she knows what she is doing. Judith is nervous and lovely. She wears her best business outfit. She expects other people, potential future clients, to be dropping by the office today.

Katy, who will be traveling with her mother, is sitting on the sofa in the living room. She has been ready for long minutes. She is slumping down on her spine, her chin digging into her chest. She looks nice, but she is very bored.

"Ready?" Grey calls, standing with his hand on the front doorknob. Judith's answer is the sound of her heels on the stairs. "All right," she says distractedly, but by that time Grey has gone out and closed the door behind him.

Judith picks up her purse, puts it down again, and picks up Katy before the baby slides completely off the sofa. "Damn," Judith says a moment later. She looks around for Grey, but realizes he is gone. She sets Katy on the sofa again and clatters back up the stairs. Katy yawns and waves her fists and rolls from side to side.

Judith returns from the nursery with the diaper bag. With practiced hands, made slightly clumsy by hurry, she removes the baby's wet diaper and pins on a new one. She walks quickly out of the room with the wet diaper and there is the sound of running water. Judith returns rubbing her hands together. A little time has passed; not much, but the house has grown almost completely silent. Judith produces the only sounds, and they are small ones. The quiet makes her glance out the window as she hoists Katy to her shoulder and collects the diaper bag and her purse. She goes quickly out the door. There are two small thumps when Judith sets down her purse and bag to lock the door behind her, then the last sounds of her footsteps, diminishing down the path. Two car doors open and close. Grey has waited for his wife. Two car engines start, and a minute later their sounds are dying in separate distances.

And now the house is still. There are few signs of the damage done to it three days earlier. The living room is dimmer at night; the twisted floor lamp has been given away and not replaced. The books are back on the shelves. Some few of their spines are cracked, but most observers would attribute that to normal wear.

Gray has cleaned up his study. The broken windowpane has been replaced, the new putty still slightly soft and undarkened. The fragments of the old window are in the trash can, along with the typewriter ribbon. The typewriter still works, after a fashion, some of the keys having a tendency to huddle close together, reluctant to leave their nest to strike the paper. Grey hasn't used the machine since the break-in. He was able to salvage all the paperwork, and has collated the pages of his manuscript, but it has stayed in one of the unwrecked desk drawers. The shattered drawer has been thrown out, leaving a gaping hole in the desk, not visible from the door.

Lucinda Carmack came to help with the cleanup, most of her efforts confined to the kitchen. Lucinda feels guilty about the Stantons. She knows she stands near the head of the long chain of events that led to the wreckage in their house. The money behind it all was hers, illegally gotten and thus a temptation to a crooked mind. Then too, Lucinda feels she should have killed Simon at her first opportunity. Instead she talked to him, scared him off, so that he has been turned aside, against her new friends. A few squares of tile in the kitchen are scarred, the starburst pattern of the scars blending into the pattern of the tiles except when the sunlight strikes them at a certain angle.

Upstairs, the nursery is the least affected room in the house. Like its occupant, it has retained its innocence.

In the master bedroom Judith and Grey have turned the mattress. With its sheets on, it appears undamaged. Its stuffing may be slowly seeping out, but it will be perfectly serviceable for a good while longer. The shower curtain in the bathroom has been replaced. The new one is more nearly transparent than the old one: a window around the shower stall. The curtain is in squares, still clearly showing where it was folded in its package. Its tangy plastic smell fills the room. The only other sign in the bathroom is one diagonal crack across the face of the mirror.

The pool table in the game room hasn't had its torn felt replaced. The collected balls congregate in the rack under the table. They have clattered together only that once since the break-in and now been still for three days.

Sunlight slants in through the French doors. The new deadbolt is locked, but French doors are notoriously difficult to protect. One good kick might fling them open. The terrace outside looks older than the rest of the house. It has already begun to develop an overworked, abandoned look. One lawn chair lies on its side. In the far corner at the front, a small puddle is still accumulated from the last rain.

Anyone watching from the terrace would see, an hour after the Stantons have left, the sheriff's patrol car pass on the road and slow. Kendrick is keeping an eye on things. He's glad to see no sign of Simon, and hopes the feud will blow over now that Simon's exacted some revenge for whatever he's mad about. The sheriff parks across the road for a few minutes, making his presence clear to any hidden watcher. But he can see the house is empty; there shouldn't be any more trouble for today at least. Kendrick looks carefully around and drives on.

Judith was the first one home. She came through the front door looking angry, but still stopped long enough to lock the deadbolt behind her. In the living room she threw her purse on the sofa and hurried past it. Katy, in the sling of her arm, watched her mother closely, taking lessons in anger. Katy had been sensing tension ever since Judith picked her up at her grandmother's house, not long after she'd been dropped off. The trip home had been uncomfortable for Katy at times but she hadn't cried. She was too watchful to cry.

Mr. Rhodes's office furniture hadn't been delivered. It was still somewhere between Chicago and Austin, probably closer to the former. Judith had spent a total of an hour on the telephone and perhaps half that much time pacing the empty office suite, with Mr. Rhodes coming in two or three times to look around perplexedly, as if Judith had suggested that his office should remain bare forever. Her last phone call had convinced her that the furniture wasn't going to appear today, and she had collected Katy and come home.

Angry as she was, she hadn't forgotten Grey's instructions. As soon as she'd seen the empty driveway she'd known she wasn't going to stay here. She was going to Lucinda's store, but first she had to change out of these clothes. She thought the house could protect her for the very few minutes that would take. The house was clean and restored, giving the illusion of sanctuary.

At the top of the stairs she set Katy on her feet and hurried into the bedroom. Her jacket was sliding off her arms as she went through the doorway, and she dropped it on the bed. She had her blouse unbuttoned and was shrugging out of it as she stepped to the closet door and pulled it open.

All this time, since coming in the front door, Judith had been keeping up a steady barrage of noise. Downstairs, on the stairs, and through the upstairs hallway, her heels had been loud and angry. Her brisk passage through the air had stirred a small, steady breeze in her own ears. She had even been muttering to herself. But silence fell now. The bedroom was carpeted and she had kicked off her shoes when she'd stepped inside it. When she opened the closet door she stopped moving and talking to herself, so those small sounds died. There were no more audible distractions. As Judith stood looking at her clothes, she heard something.

She closed her eyes. A pained expression settled on her face. She pulled her blouse back on and held it clutched at her throat for a moment. When she turned quickly she saw Katy in the doorway, and beckoned the baby to her. She stepped into flat shoes and again heard a noise from downstairs, too faint to recognize.

She'd been a fool to stop here. Hadn't she spent enough terrified moments in this house already? When she turned around, the house seemed to have crumbled into the disorder of three days before. New locks and books standing straight on their shelves didn't mean safety.

Katy touched her leg, looking up at her with wide eyes. Judith gave her a feeble smile. She walked to the bed and Katy followed her. Judith sat and put a hand on Katy's head as she picked up the phone. She was already reaching for the buttons when she realized there was no dial tone. She held it against her ear, waiting, but the instrument remained dead and useless.

She put a finger to her lips, then picked up the baby and stepped quickly to the doorway. She had to be more careful in the uncarpeted hall. After two steps she slipped the shoes off and continued, hurrying. She hadn't heard a door or window opening, so she was still alone in the house.

Unless he'd already been inside when she'd arrived.

That thought struck her when she was halfway down the stairs. She stopped so abruptly her stocking feet almost slid off the step. She stood paralyzed for a long minute, until Katy looked at her with her mouth slowly opening to cry. Judith shook her head and started silently down the stairs again. When she was far enough down she stopped to peer over the railing into the living room. It, at least, was empty. She could see it all from this vantage. No one was staring in the window.

Judith was even more careful coming down the last few stairs. Katy was mercifully silent. Judith crossed the living room, wincing with every step, and came safely to the hall doorway. Slowly, terribly slowly, she leaned out into the front hall.

It was empty. Judith took three fast steps to the front door, panic rising in her throat when she was nearly free of the house. It almost came out as a scream when she turned the handle and pulled. The door was locked tight, she couldn't open it without a key, and her keys were in her purse on the sofa.

The burst of fear left her calm in its aftermath. She stood with her hand on the doorknob and breathed deeply. Katy touched her face. Judith shook off the hand and walked quickly back into the living room, safe behind a determined expression. Every piece of furniture looked crouched, disguised, but the room was still empty. That fact made Judith pause when she picked up her purse. Quiet as she'd been, Simon should have heard her by now if he was in the house. She stood still, letting her senses creep through the house, until she was convinced she was alone.

Which meant that he was outside. Judith set Katy down on the sofa and went to the window. The view from it remained empty, and even when she flattened her face against the pane she could see no one crouching under the window or flattened against the wall beside it. She had a giddy moment of relief. Maybe she was alone, panicked by nothing. But she didn't let the emotion run away with her. She walked past Katy again, the baby watching her soberly. She was such a good baby, quiet when she had to be, not easily frightened. Judith wondered if she could hide her somewhere.

She returned to the front door and looked through the peephole. No one. But the peephole didn't afford a 360-degree angle. Judith tried looking down, but that showed her nothing. And the front door stood in a right angle, so he could have been hiding around the corner, outside and to her left.

Judith returned to the living room, chewing on her lip. She could see the car, hardly thirty feet away. The ready car, waiting to carry her away. She should have been able to fly to it from here.

She stopped chewing and stared at the car again. She blinked twice, digesting her new idea. She didn't like it, didn't like any of the alternatives. But she couldn't delay any longer. All the windows of the house were easy to shatter. She wasn't safe where she was.

With Katy on her hip and her purse in that hand, she stood at the window again. It afforded the widest empty view. She could see that no one was near it. Clenching her teeth, she unlocked it. Then, slowly again, eyes slitted, she raised it. It stuck after a few inches. She shifted Katy to the other hip and tried again. The window slid smoothly up.

Now she was completely unsafe. But the front door couldn't be seen from this window, and vice versa. If Simon were crouched there or around the far corner, she might—

Taking a deep breath and smiling at Katy to show it was all in fun, she stepped out. It was farther down to the ground than she'd expected; she almost fell. But she steadied herself and pulled her other leg out.

Then she ran like hell. Simon was everywhere. Coming from his position at the front door, coming through the window behind her, dropping off the roof onto her shoulders. The real danger was that he was hiding behind the corner of the house she had to run past to reach the car. She speeded up as she approached, swerving aside. She shifted the baby in her arms and her blouse flapped open. Rocks bruised the unprotected soles of her feet. Her ankle twisted and she recovered quickly, grabbing Katy with both hands.

As she ran past the corner she shrieked from sheer tension. There was no one there. She ran faster, feeling fingers falling on her shoulder. Silence was gone. Wherever Simon was hiding, he knew where she was, and he would be much faster. She veered around the front of the car and back to the car door. Thank God she'd left the door unlocked. She pulled it open, expecting to be caught at that moment. But she felt enormously strong now. She was almost inside the car, safe again. She could shake off a hand if it caught her now, maybe even slam it in the door. She flung herself inside, slammed the door, and locked it. She dropped Katy to the seat beside her and laughed. Katy laughed too. Great fun. Judith sat taking deep breaths. Of course there was no one hammering on the door, no one to be seen at all. She would arrive at Lucinda's looking frayed and torn, and for silliness. She smiled at Katy and fumbled through her purse for the car keys.

Simon rose off the floorboards behind her. She felt the movement and was already screaming before she saw his face in the rearview mirror. Katy shrieked too, unable to see the danger.

She thought he might leave the baby in the car. That idea made Judith resist less when he pulled her over the seat and out his back door. She fell against him, felt his breath on her ear and his forearm across her neck, and she screamed again, loudly enough to cover Katy's thin voice. But when they were out of the car he pushed Judith, hard enough to throw her down on the hood, then unlocked the driver's door and reached in to take Katy. Katy continued to wail as he carried her across his shoulder, more like a sack than a baby. He strode toward the house and Judith hurried after him, leaning forward, her upturned palms below his back. Katy reached for her and Judith grasped the baby's hands, but Simon held her relentlessly, and rather than pull the baby between them Judith just held onto her hands, protecting her against a fall. She stubbed her toe hard against a rock and stumbled, almost falling, releasing Katy's hands, falling behind.

"Please." She hurried to catch up, hopping the first step or two. "Let me have her."

Surprisingly, he did. At the front door Simon thrust the baby into Judith's arms, and it was so unexpected that for a moment she felt grateful to him. She hugged the baby tightly and Katy clutched a fistful of her hair. Judith almost started crying. She just stood there holding the baby, not trying to run while Simon's head was turned. She wouldn't have gotten far. She hoped for the sound of a car, but they were surrounded by a miles-wide stillness.

Simon turned the doorknob and pushed on the door ineffectually. He rattled the knob, then stepped back and kicked it. Then again, drawing his knee back almost to his chest and hitting the door with his heel. And again. He hadn't looked at Judith since their eyes had met in the rearview mirror, but she winced every time the door shivered under his foot. He wasn't exhausting his rage, he was building it. She prayed for the door to give way. She felt the impact of the kicks on her own body.

The door held. When Simon glared at her she shrank away, raising a forearm and saying, "No." She said "No" again when he grabbed her upper arm and dragged her along the front of the house.

"Where's your keys?"

"The car."

But before they got there they passed the open window. He looked at Judith curiously and, still holding her arm, reached toward her with the other hand. She thought he was offering to help her across the sill, but he was taking Katy. She was in his arms before Judith knew his intention. When she reached for the baby he stepped through the window and was almost immediately out of her sight.

Judith banged her shin on the sill and fell to the floor when she had crossed over it. The thought that she could escape hadn't occurred to her. She was quickly on her feet and moving through the dim room, calling. Sunspots flared at the edges of her vision.

"Where are you? Simon!" It was the first time she had ever addressed him. She ran out the back of the living room into the hall, skidded on the hardwood floor, and righted herself against the wall. It seemed they had been out of her sight for minutes, and she had no idea what he intended. It was so easy to hurt a baby.

They were in the study. Simon was walking along the wall, hitting it at intervals with his fist. Katy sat in the crook of his other arm and he was bouncing her minutely, perhaps unconsciously. Katy had stopped crying. She stared at Simon with a disapproval tempered by fascination. He was the strangest thing she'd ever seen. Her gaze seemed to be caught on the ear that was partially hidden behind unkempt black hair. But every time his fist hit the wall her head jerked around to look at it. Then she would turn again to his ear, for explanation.

Judith walked cautiously toward them, took Katy under the arms, and tried to lift her away. But Simon shook her off and shifted the baby to his other arm. He scarcely seemed aware that he was holding her. "Where is it?" he mumbled. Then louder: "Where is it?"

"What?" Judith hadn't realized he was talking to her.

He stopped hitting the wall and turned to her. The baby was caught between them, Judith taking her arms again. Simon distractedly let himself be robbed of her. He stared at Judith while she cooed to Katy and wiped her chin. It was some seconds before she looked at him again.

"I wonder if you know," he said musingly. Judith only looked at him. Simon looked back at her, a long speculative stare that finally turned Judith's gaze aside. Simon shrugged fatalistically. "Dudn't matter."

Judith stepped back, but before she could take another step he was hurrying toward her. He was almost past her when his fingers dug into her arm again.

He dragged her upstairs, her feet skittering for balance, trying to resist his pull and keep Katy upright in her arms. Simon glanced into the nursery, said, "This'll do," and took them inside.

Frilliness in the nursery was confined to the yellow curtains. They hung limply, almost to the window seat. The furniture consisted of the baby bed and a straight-backed chair with arms. Simon pushed Judith into the chair and took Katy away from her. Judith hung on, but released the baby when he gave her a warning look. She couldn't protect Katy, could only anger him. He set Katy on the window seat and the baby seemed to like it there. She leaned forward to look over the edge and Judith rose toward her. Simon pushed her back into the chair.

He turned to the closet. Judith looked at the door, the window, at Katy. Judith was leaning forward, her hands on the arms of the chair, but there was nowhere to go. She leaned back again, feeling her pains. Her legs ached in too many spots to count. She rubbed her arm, where she could almost feel the flesh still indented from his grip.

Simon turned back to her. Her blouse was still unbuttoned, and Judith instinctively held it closed with her hand, but she was afraid of what that might suggest to him, and she lowered her hand again, trying to look unprovocative. The nursery closet held, besides Katy's clothes, old dresses and blouses of Judith's. Simon had pulled two or three off their hangers. He looked at Judith as he tore one down its full length, then gripped the fabric to tear again.

Judith looked down at her hands resting on the chair arms, jerked them away, and stood up. Simon lowered his hands and took one step toward her. She didn't sit again until he reached toward her. She sank down before he could touch her. Simon stood close in front of her as he finished tearing the dress into strips.

He tied her left hand first. Judith pulled the right one away when he reached for it. "Please," she said again. "What do you want?" He pulled her hand firmly down and tied it to the arm of the chair. When he squatted to tie her feet to the legs his hair brushed her knee. She drew her leg aside. Simon saw the movement and looked up at her, his face at her knees. He sneered.

"That's right, try ta keep me from touchin' your pretty white skin. You might git dirty." He put his hands on her knees to raise himself and kept his hands there as he leaned forward to speak into her face. "Don't you realize yet that I own you? Don't you know that?" He lifted his hands off her knees and raised them the length of her body, the hands moving fast, almost but not quite touching her. She was pressed against the back of the chair, her head turned aside from his breath. One of his hands touched her neck and the collar of her blouse before he leaned back away from her.

"But I think you might be good for something besides that. What else you think you might be good for? Hmm?"

She shook her head.

"You cain't imagine? Well—" He stood all the way up, back another step. "You think you might be good for sendin' a message to your husband?"

She stared up at him. "I'll tell him anything you want."

He smiled at her naiveté. "I don't mean *take* a message," he said. He reached behind his back and his hand emerged with a knife. "I mean *be* a message."

A bone-handled hunting knife, well-kept, its edge honed down to infinity. Simon let it hang between them for a moment, offering it for admiration. He leaned toward her, advancing the knife. She didn't turn away from it, didn't offer her neck.

"Don't," she said. "Don't." Talking rapidly. "This is a terrible idea. They'll know you did this and they'll get you."

"I know they'll know. That's the point. *He'll* know."

He stopped moving the knife toward her and gave her that appraising look again. "Unless you got a better idea? Some other kinda message we could give 'im?"

Judith couldn't bring herself to speak. He looked at her and read her mind. Anger flared in his eyes but his voice was still amiable. "Well, then. Back to this." He came toward her again.

"But it won't do you any good. I don't know anything. I'd tell you. . . . You'll be back in prison. You just got out, you don't want to go right back again, do you? Oh God."

He laid the knife against her cheek. The edge was so sharp, so cold that she felt as if she were bleeding the instant it touched her.

"That's what I want him to know." Simon's voice was soft, loverlike. "I know he's already trying to send me back. Right this minute, isn't he?"

"No."

"Hush now. Don't lie to me."

The knife moved, gently. She was sure she was bleeding now.

"That's what I want him to know. I can do anything I want, but you cain't hurt me. You can get my parole revoked. You can set the law on me for this here. I'll just hide out. I won't be givin' up anything, 'cause he's already stole everything I had. See? And I'll get y'all. I won't have anything better to do than follow you until I get my chance. Won't nothin' protect you. Cops, locks. You'll have to go live in the jail. Right in the cell. And one day the cop guardin' you'll get bored, or go out for lunch, or hear somethin' else he has to run check on. And as soon as he walks out the door I'll walk in."

"I don't have your money!"

"I don't think you do." He laid the knife against her other cheek, vertically this time. The knife was so sharp there was little pain, but the feel of her skin parting under it was terrifying. Judith was crying. The salty tears stung when they reached the cuts. It seemed to her the blood was welling freely down her face. "You look like a red Indian on the warpath," Simon said judiciously.

He suddenly stood and tossed the knife away behind him. It landed on the window seat, next to Katy. "Katy!" Judith said sharply as the baby bent curiously over the blade. Simon's lazy attention turned to the window seat. He looked back at Judith, considering.

"I don't think you'll want to see any more."

He bent to the rags around his feet, found another strip, and raised it to her face. She shrieked and twisted her head quickly back and forth. Simon grabbed her neck, forced her head back, and stuffed the cloth in her mouth instead. He bent quickly and found another strip to tie around her head, holding the first rag in place.

"Okay, you can watch, but no more of that racket."

He picked up Katy in one hand and the knife in the other. "Here, baby. Come on, baby. You want this? You sure?"

Katy still watched the shiny knife, and reached for it when Simon offered it. She grabbed it by the blade and immediately dropped it and started screaming.

"Ahhh. You just got to know how to hold it. Here." He stooped and retrieved the knife. Offering the handle this time, he induced Katy to take it. She held the point toward her face, her tongue playing at her lips. "There you go," Simon said.

He held the baby in the crook of one arm and studied her. His other hand roamed slowly over her body, rearranging her silky strands of hair, caressing her forearm. He seemed fascinated with the baby's soft skin. Judith squirmed in her chair, twisting her wrists, but that only caused the rags to cut more deeply into her skin. Whatever she tried to say was only a mumble through her gag. She stared at Simon, eyes pleading to bargain.

As both of them watched the baby Simon walked slowly behind Judith. She twisted her head to keep him in sight, but he stood directly behind her, so that she couldn't get a clear angle. "Careful now," she heard Simon warn Katy. "Don't drop it on your momma's head."

Judith's continued twisting and craning brought Simon's attention. He laid a hand on her hair and she couldn't shake it off. She couldn't see if he was looking at her or at Katy, but she knew the next time he spoke it was to her.

"Now what's the matter? Cain't stand to be ignored, can you? All right."

He stepped forward so that the back of her head rested against his crotch. She strained forward, but he held her in place. She slipped free when he moved his hand, but now the hand pursued her, fingers going into her ear, the hand sliding down her neck.

Katy cried out, and the knife fell against Judith's head and then to the floor.

"What did you do now?" Simon's hand left Judith. Katy continued to cry. "My goodness, I bet that hurts. We'd better give the knife back to your momma."

Judith heard Katy deposited in the bed behind her. The baby continued to cry. Simon stooped, retrieved the knife, and brought it to Judith's face again.

"Maybe I'm makin' a mistake," he said musingly. "Maybe after your husband sees you like this he won't even care what happens to you anymore. You think if I make you ugly enough you might even get interested in an ugly old thing like me?"

He was squatting in front of her, eyes level with Judith's. He looked at her seriously for a moment, then his eyes went slowly downward. With his left hand he opened her blouse wider. Judith was crying again. She closed her eyes when he touched her. His fingers were crusty. She thought they must be leaving a trail as he caressed slowly down from her neck toward her breast.

"But you wouldn't like it down in the dirt with the common folk, would you?" he said softly. "Or maybe you would. Be an interestin' change, wouldn't it?"

She opened her eyes again. He was so close she could hear and see and smell nothing else. She twisted frantically, but there was no escape. She didn't know which was worse, the knife or his hand. Her scream was trapped somewhere in her throat.

They both heard the sound of a car on the gravel driveway below. Judith's head jerked toward the window, then she turned back to Simon. They stared at each other. The relief

Judith had felt vanished as she thought of Grey unknowingly walking into the house.

"Oh my," Simon said quietly. "The whole family together again. Now, you won't forget my message, will you? Just let me help you remember." He brought the knife lower.

•

Grey frowned when he saw Judith's car in the driveway. It wasn't safe for her to be here alone. Simon wasn't stationed across the road, but he might still be around. Grey got out of the car and walked down the driveway toward the back of the house, wanting to see if Simon was anywhere in the fields behind the house. He didn't see anything. But as he turned the corner into the backyard he glimpsed something and turned back. Simon was sauntering across the road, away from the house. But he hadn't been in sight a moment before. Grey didn't give him a second look. He ran to the back door, had a little trouble with the new lock, but finally got it open and ran into the kitchen.

"Judith!" he shouted. There was no answer and he didn't hear Katy either. Grey ran down the short hallway to the empty living room, calling their names again. He saw that one of the living room windows was standing open. He gave it one horrified look and flung himself up the stairs, shouting into the silence.

# 14

"WHAT ARE YOU GOING TO DO?"

Grey drove.

A few miles later she asked again, "What are you going to do?"

"Take you home," he said this time.

"And then?"

Grey drove. He had been over this road only the day before, and many times in the past months. He no longer saw the road. The muscles in his arms shifted the wheel without his interference.

"Tell me what you're going to do, Grey."

Judith's voice sounded odd. When Grey glanced at her she met his eyes for only a moment, then looked away. She imagined that her face looked worse than it did. There was only a thin red line on each cheek, one vertical, one horizontal. They had hardly bled, but they stood out on her pale skin. They were markers, indications showing where the face could be broken apart. Judith kept her face as still as possible, hardly moving her lips when she spoke. The voice that emerged sounded easily breakable itself.

The cut under her chin had bled more copiously. It was an inch long, below her jawline and slightly to her left, at the very top of her neck. Another marker. Grey had cleaned it and Judith had held a cotton swab to the cut while Grey had packed her suitcase. She had discarded the swab now, but a few wisps from it clung to the cut as if seeping out of it: fragile Judith bleeding thin white blood. Whenever he looked at her Grey was reminded of the smaller cut under his own chin. He resisted touching it.

"Are you going to call the police?"

"No."

"Why not? This is it, Grey. There's no question about this. I'll testify and he'll be right back in prison."

Grey shook his head. "He was right. What he told you was the truth. There's no way for us to protect ourselves from him. If we go to the police he'll just fade away until they get tired of looking for him. And in the meantime we'll be staring at the ceiling every night, with Katy between us, wondering what every noise is."

"They'll catch him. He's not a ghost. We can't start ascribing supernatural powers to him just because—"

Grey glanced in the rearview mirror. Katy sat very still in her seat, watching them, listening as if she could understand. Her eyes were drawn to her mother's neck every time Judith turned her head.

"What if they do catch him? They'll revoke his parole and send him back. To finish an eight-year sentence he's already served three years of. He might not get granted another parole, but even if he doesn't, where do you think he'll go when he gets out?"

"Five years from now? I can't worry that far in advance. Maybe we'll all be dead by then."

The landscape flowed on. They passed a house, then two more on the opposite side of the road. Grey found himself studying those houses more closely than he ever had before. He wondered who lived in them.

"What if we are alive?" he said. "We'll be five years older, Katy will be. He'll be five years more bitter."

"We'll move." Judith was turned sideways in her seat, but she didn't reach to touch him. Her voice was cajoling now; she was the one making light of her injuries. Grey's voice was cold.

"Where? To Austin? Do you think that will be far enough? Dallas? Out of the state? How far will we have to go for you to feel safe?"

She opened her mouth, then let it close when no answer came. "What else can we do?" she finally asked. Grey didn't answer that. They drove the rest of the way to her parents' house in silence. Grey parked in front and turned off the engine. They continued to sit, feeling the heat accumulating in the car.

Judith stirred and looked at Katy. "Well. Come on."

"Just you two. I'm going back."

"Grey." Judith made two imperative syllables out of the name. He continued to look out the windshield. Judith's back was to the house, and she didn't turn to look at it. In peripheral vision Grey saw the front door open, saw Judith's mother standing quizzically, looking at the closed car.

"Don't worry," he said. "I'm not going to get hurt and I'm not going to get into trouble. I'm just going to end it."

"How?"

After a pause he said again, "Don't worry."

There was a longer pause. Judith glanced at her mother but didn't wave. Her wandering gaze finally held on Grey's averted face.

"You know what I wish?" she said. "I wish you *had* taken his money, so you could just give it back to him."

Grey didn't answer. He pointed with his chin at her waiting mother. "All right," Judith finally said. "Come on, Katy, we're going to see Grandma."

She opened both doors on her side of the car, got out, and reached in for the baby. Grey got out to help with the bags, and Judith set Katy on her feet. The baby toddled up the sidewalk to meet her grandmother. From that distance, Judith's mother couldn't see the cuts on Judith's face, but she looked at the couple quizzically. Judith and Grey faced each other, and before the pause could grow longer Grey stepped forward and held her. Her arms were tight against his back.

"I'll call you," he said. "Don't worry."

"That's a stupid thing to say." She was crying without being noisy about it.

Grey shrugged, kissed her quickly, and hurried away.

Grey drove quickly to a nearby mall, glancing from the setting sun to his watch. There was still time. On weekdays his savings bank stayed open until seven.

He took the first parking place he saw and ran through the lot, an object of attention in the midst of the slow traffic of cars and pedestrians. He slowed to a fast walk inside the mall, the air conditioning cooling the sweat on his back. At the savings and loan he stood behind an elderly woman who took an inordinate amount of time to figure the interest on her certificate of deposit. When Grey's turn came to step to the counter the clerk smiled from a sense of duty, Grey from habit.

"I'd like to make a withdrawal," he said.

# 15

GREY SAT IN THE WELL-LIGHTED LIVING ROOM, TURNING the pages of the book in his lap. The book seemed to hold his interest; he turned the pages at a normal rate. Occasionally he did look up, but when he did he looked around the room, at the clock, toward the ceiling—not out the living room window. Two or three times during the evening he stood up, stretched, and walked to the kitchen, passing several windows.

Long before midnight he set the book aside and yawned, then stood and turned off the light. In the sudden darkness the window was the only sight in the world, and Grey's body the deepest blackness. He shuffled out of the room to check the front door and then the back, making sure both were unlocked. At the same slow pace he climbed to his bedroom, lights flaring ahead of him and dimming out after he passed. He undressed methodically, hanging up his clothes, and donned pajamas. When he sat on the edge of the bed he looked at the clock, and his gaze passed over the phone. He couldn't keep his promise to call Judith because the line was still cut somewhere outside.

Grey turned off the last light in the house and stretched out supine on the bed, arms angled away from his sides. He breathed slowly, easily.

In the morning he rose, dressed, and returned to the living room. Today he kept himself busier. He ran the vacuum cleaner over the rug, rearranged the books, dusted a little, continually moving through the room and back and forth to the kitchen. At noon he made himself a sandwich and ate it standing up at the counter, not listening to a radio or reading while he ate: a man whose business was chewing.

After lunch he retired to his study and read the incomplete manuscript of his book. He smiled occasionally, but more often read with a neutral expression, and he didn't make any marks in the manuscript. Toward the end there was a page missing. Grey looked through the other papers he'd stored in the desk but couldn't find the missing page. He sat back in his chair by the window and read again the broken sentences surrounding the lost page, trying to reconstruct the gap. But in the end he returned the manuscript to the desk without writing anything.

It was late afternoon before he heard something. The susurrus of an approaching car grew louder as it slowed and crunched into the driveway. Grey rose quickly and hurried to the living room. From there he glimpsed the sheriff's car, and stepped out of sight into the hallway behind the front door. He was at the peephole when the sheriff's image filled it.

The sheriff rang the bell. Grey didn't move, even when the bell sounded again. When Kendrick knocked loudly on the door he rattled the panel an inch from Grey's forehead. Grey didn't flinch. He watched the sheriff step back, frown, turn to look at whatever was visible from the front of the house. He took a step toward his car, then turned back and stepped up on the porch again. His hand went to the doorknob. Inside, Grey's did the same. On opposite sides of the door they hesitated, their hands hovering around the doorknobs. Then the sheriff's hand rose to knock on the door again, halfheartedly, before he strode away to his car. Grey moved to the living room to watch it ride out of sight. Then he returned to the front door and tried the knob. It turned easily; the door slipped free of its frame. Leaving it ajar, Grey crossed the living room to the study.

An hour or more later—he wasn't wearing a watch—when he heard a footstep in the living room, Grey snapped on the light over his head.

Dusk had invaded the house. Grey looked around the room at his desk, his filing cabinet, his bookshelves, took a deep breath, and stood up. He felt very calm, and a little tired. His eyes closed slowly, and opened when a rifle barrel pushed the door further open.

"Come in," he said, and Simon stepped distrustfully into the room.

"If you think that sheriff's gonna save you, you got another think comin'. I followed him all the way to the main road, and he went toward town. And there ain't nobody else around. I been out there all day."

"I know," Grey said.

"Not much of a trap," Simon sniffed.

"It's not a trap at all." Grey spread his arms. "I wanted to see you. Come in."

Arms still invitingly open, Grey took the few steps to the door and pulled it wide. As he came that close, Simon raised the rifle barrel, intending it only for menace. But by then Grey was too close, so that the rifle was an awkward length between them. Grey's hand moved suddenly from the door to the rifle barrel, twisting it aside. Simon grabbed the stock with both hands, as Grey had planned. Grey stepped even closer and drove his fist deep into Simon's belly.

Simon gasped and bent, but he didn't let go of the gun. Grey took it in both hands and twisted it almost in a full circle, feeling the resistance of Simon's finger bones caught in the trigger guard. Simon screamed and jerked free. He was upright again. Grey had plenty of time to propel his fist from the level of his waist to Simon's jaw. Simon saw it coming the last few inches but was too stunned to duck back. Grey hit him as hard as he could, feeling the tension of weeks released with the blow. Simon rebounded from the doorframe and Grey caught him and pushed him toward the chair beside the desk. Then it was Simon looking up fearfully and Grey standing over him with the rifle. This wasn't the .22 Simon had carried before, it was a larger gun, with a bolt action. It was a satisfying weight in Grey's hands. Simon didn't move. Grey breathed hard, staring at him, then raised the rifle and threw it across the room, to the opposite side of the desk.

Simon watched it fall, and they both listened. When Simon looked back, he saw that he was being dared to move. He stayed in the chair, watching Grey with obvious bafflement.

"I wanted to prove a point to you," Grey said. "You're not any stronger than I am. You've just been more willing to fight than I've been. *Have been.*"

"What now?" Simon said. He kept his eyes carefully away from the direction in which the rifle lay. Grey could read his expression.

"Now this." Grey turned his back on Simon

and walked to the bookcase. When he turned back, Simon was still in the chair. "How much money do you think I stole from you?" Grey asked.

Simon just stared at him. He could see that there was a plan at work here, but he didn't know what his part in it was.

"This much?" Grey said. He reached behind some books and pulled out a wrapped stack of bills. He tossed them at Simon, who caught them against his chest and turned them to read the wrapper that said five hundred dollars. After a moment of holding them and staring at Grey, he shook his head minutely.

"More? Was it this much?" Grey reached behind a second shelf and pulled out a similarly wrapped stack of bills. They too arced toward the thief in the chair beside the desk. Simon caught them, glanced quickly at the identifying figure and held them with the others. "More," he said sullenly.

"Really?" Grey said. He stood with one hand on his hip, the other resting lightly on books, half-turned away from Simon. After a moment he moved along the shelves. Simon's eyes followed him closely.

Grey reached behind books and brought out another five-hundred-dollar package. He shook it slightly in his hand, watching the bills flap, then tossed it to Simon as well.

Simon caught it with the other two, and held the fifteen hundred dollars clutched against his stomach. His attention didn't flicker from Grey.

"Is that enough?" Grey said quietly. "I hope it wasn't more than fifteen hundred dollars."

"What's three years of my life worth?" Simon said, almost whining.

"Not much." Grey moved along the bookcase. "What's the rest of your life worth to you?"

"What?"

"I hope that's as much money as you lost," Grey continued. He reached behind another set of books, pulled out the pistol, and pointed it at Simon's face. "—because I'm going to kill you if you're not satisfied with that."

Simon leaped backward in his chair. The back stopped him and tipped him forward again. One of the packages of bills came loose and slid down to his lap, where Simon caught it, still holding the others against his chest. He sat there as if shielding his vitals with money.

Grey cocked the hammer of the pistol. "Oh Jesus," Simon said. He stretched a hand out in front of him. It still held a packet of bills, and suddenly realizing that the sight of them in his possession might offend his captor, Simon dropped the packet to the floor. "Wait," he said. "Wait, wait a minute." His head was lowered.

Grey stepped closer to him. There was more

expression in the tension of the hand holding the pistol than there was on Grey's face.

"Look up. Look at me. All right. Do you understand? If you ever come back here, I'll kill you. Just the sight of you, that's all it will take." The pistol was very close to Simon's face and hands. It would have been easy for him to lunge for it. Grey's hand was aware of that. It kept making tiny jerks upward. Simon's head twitched in time to the movement. His eyes stayed on the gun.

"Take the money," Grey said. "Take it. I want you to." He kicked the dropped packet toward Simon's feet. "You take that money and you'll have everything you want. There won't be any more reason for this. If you wanted more than that, forget it. That's all you'll ever get, no matter what. Isn't it better to have this much than to be dead?"

Grey waited for an answer and Simon finally nodded. His fingernails were tearing at the wrapper around one of the packets.

"You believe me? That I'll kill you if you give me the slightest excuse? God, when I think—" There was no need to feign this anger. Grey's face was filled with blood. For the first time he had let himself dwell for a moment on the thought of Simon inside this house with Judith and Katy. He raised the gun higher, to a dominating position above Simon's skull. He stopped to swallow and remained silent. It would be better to kill him now, he was thinking, not take any chances.

The silence was terrifying to Simon. He knew just what Grey was thinking. Simon had unconsciously pushed his chair back until it was behind the level of the desk, still beside it. Grey had followed him. Simon watched the pistol closely but didn't move to defend himself.

The air grew cooler. Grey stepped back and lowered the gun to his side. "Take the money and get out of here," he said wearily. He waved the pistol toward the door. Simon's breath eased too, but he didn't move.

"Go on, hurry up."

Simon reached down for the five hundred dollars at his feet, but when he straightened up his face had become calculating again. He drew his feet under him but didn't stand.

"What are you waiting for?" Grey grew mad again, and when he waved the pistol Simon flinched.

"I know what you're doin'," he whined. "It *is* a trap. If I try ta walk out of here you're gonna shoot me."

Grey exhaled loudly. "God. Get out! Look. Look, I'll uncock the pistol. See? I'm lowering the hammer slowly." He'd damned well better lower it slowly. He didn't want the hammer falling on the empty chamber. "All right? Are you satisfied?"

Simon shook his head. "You're gonna shoot me in the back and say I was robbin' you." Simon pushed his chair back further.

"I don't know how I can convince you. I already told you I'll kill you if I see you again. If I was going to do it now I would've already done it." This wasn't working right. Grey wanted him out, fast. His pistol felt very light.

Simon whined, "I hadn't done nothin' to you, and you were gonna have 'em take back my parole. It's not fair." His eyes slithered across Grey's set face. "Can I take my rifle?"

"Of course not."

Grey glanced at the rifle, as Simon had. When Grey turned away, Simon suddenly threw at him the packet of money whose band he'd torn off. Before it struck, Simon dived out of his chair, behind the desk, scrambling toward the rifle.

"Stop! I'll shoot!" Grey shouted helplessly. A curtain of money fluttered in the air. Grey took a step toward the rifle, but Simon was already there. Grey threw the useless, unloaded pistol and plummeted toward the door. He was out of the room before Simon could fire, but there were heavy footsteps behind him.

His plan had seemed so good. Hurt Simon, gratify his greed, then threaten his life. It had worked for Lucinda Carmack. But her threat had been real. He should have bought bullets with the pistol. But it hadn't been part of his plan to run the risk of going to prison for shooting Simon. Using an unloaded gun wouldn't subject him to the temptation of killing his tormentor, he had reasoned. He hadn't counted on putting his own life in jeopardy.

Grey ran down the short hallway past the kitchen doorway and turned the corner into the longer hallway. The front door was ahead of him, closed. He was almost there, but how many extra seconds would it take to get that far and pull the door open? He could feel Simon behind him. He wanted to be out of sight as quickly as possible. When he came to the living room doorway he ducked through it. He had been right. A bullet smacked into the front door just after he dodged aside.

He was in the living room, and it seemed so empty. As he passed the coffee table he reached for a vase and flung it back over his shoulder. He heard it shatter somewhere in the vicinity of the doorway. And since he didn't hear another shot immediately, he decided the vase must have made Simon hesitate before rushing headlong into the room after him. Grey scrambled onto the sofa and over it, feeling it tip under him and fall heavily onto its back as he vaulted clear.

Simon had still not entered the room and Grey pulled up short at the archway at the back of the living room, the one that led back into the short hallway between the study and the kitchen. He hated to stop running, he still felt pursued, but Simon could be waiting for him around that corner. Grey could run up the stairs instead, but that would mean taking a few steps back into the living room to the foot of the stairs, and if Simon suddenly stepped into the room, Grey would be helplessly exposed. Terribly slowly, ready to leap back, Grey peeked around the corner. The short hallway was empty. Simon could have kept both hallways covered by staying at the corner, but he hadn't realized that yet. Grey waited, nerves screeching, until the rifle barrel poked into the living room from the far doorway, the one by the front door. As soon as it appeared Grey stepped quietly through his own doorway and tiptoed to the kitchen doorway. The gloom was relieved there. It was much brighter outside than in the interior of the house. Maybe there was a moon outside. Something threw dim light through the windows.

That light made Grey nervous, and when he heard a noise in the living room he started running again. But as he thudded through the kitchen, making enough noise to betray his whereabouts, he wondered suddenly if he'd be any safer outside. He couldn't remember where his car keys were, and he had no guarantee that Simon hadn't done something to the car. His only escape would be on foot, and that was no safety at all. His lead on Simon wasn't long enough for him to be out of sight before Simon was after him. He'd have to duck around a corner of the house and keep circling out of Simon's sight, in a hide-and-seek in which all the advantages would be Simon's.

All this passed through his mind instantly as he ran toward the back door. When he got to it he yanked it open, slamming it loudly back against the wall, then took two quick steps backward into the closet-size pantry. He pulled the door to and stood there in total darkness. There was a rack of knives beside the door, but he reached for them very, very slowly. He would rather be unarmed than knock something over in the dark.

Heavy footsteps outside on the linoleum, and Simon's breath coming in curses. Grey shook once and froze. His hand had just found the handle of a knife. He suddenly found himself enraged, enveloped by the killing madness of an animal at the point of death. In his mind was an image of Judith and Katy alone in this house, with Grey dead and Simon still alive. That was the one thing he couldn't let happen. His hand tightened on the handle of the knife. When the door opened he would be on Simon so fast the two of them would die together. Grey was all fury now, no more logic; he waited eagerly for the pantry door to open. He had to choke back a challenging growl.

The footsteps pounded past his hiding place, hesitated, and diminished.

In one exhalation Grey lost his maddened bloodlust. It had been an instinctive defense and not a very good one. He'd be dead now if Simon had opened the pantry door.

What now? He couldn't stay here until Simon gave up or was scared off. But was there any better sanctuary? He stood in the lightening darkness until he had a new plan. He checked his pockets and found his house key. He could lock Simon out, which wouldn't be much of a defense, but would delay Simon and make him concentrate his efforts at one spot, while Grey made his escape at another. Right now he had no idea where Simon had gone. He had to reconnoiter. If he locked both front and back doors, it would force Simon to break in noisily, giving away his location. In the meantime, Grey would go up to the terrace and try to spot him. Maybe he could even drop something on him, knock him unconscious long enough to get the rifle.

He felt very weak in the aftermath of his fear and rage. Everything inside him had evaporated. It would be no trouble to move quietly. He almost believed he could float through the closed door.

He opened it slowly, gripping the knife. Simon could be just outside the back door, close enough for a shot.

He wasn't. Grey slipped out of the pantry and, staying close to the wall, surveyed the backyard. There was no sign of Simon. That might be bad, but for the moment Grey was grateful for it. He swung the back door silently closed and locked it. That done, he backed away quickly. The locked door was a clear sign of his presence. He wanted to get away from it.

He backed up for several feet, keeping watch out the kitchen window and the panes of glass in the back door. The landscape remained clear. At the doorway he turned, his nerves jumping suddenly with the idea that someone was behind him. But the hall was clear when he stepped into it, its dimness welcome after the bright kitchen.

He took four steps to the left and was at the hallway that led straight to the front door. That door was still closed. He couldn't pick out the spot where the bullet had struck. He moved slowly down the hall, into deeper blackness. As soon as he had the front door locked he would feel safe again. Ridiculous, but the images of locked doors still held the power to comfort, even after they'd proven ineffectual time and again. The knife was in Grey's right hand, the key in his left. He smiled. When he was still four feet away, the front door opened.

Grey screamed and threw himself against it. The door hit him in the face, but he didn't notice as his weight fell against it, forcing the door back.

But the door wouldn't fit its frame anymore. Something was wrong. Grey ran his hands frantically around the edges before looking down. The toe of a boot was caught between the door and the frame.

Grey was still yelling, and he realized that Simon was too. The door held thinly between them, lodged on the boot. Simon's agonized strength was beginning to force the door open. Grey leaned into it, but the contest was wavering against him. His feet skidded on the slick floor.

He was going down. He fell, and the door came open another few inches. The boot pressed in toward him. Grey's back was to the door, still impeding its opening. With a wild shriek, he stabbed the knife deep into the top of the boot. The tough leather slowed it, but he felt the point break skin and embed itself in bone.

Simon screamed. Grey heard the rifle clatter to the porch. He threw himself back against the door with renewed energy, almost catching his own fingers when the door slammed. He instantly turned the old lock, then fumbled out his key and locked the deadbolt.

He scrambled up. No time to rest. He had nothing now, his knife was gone. He started down the hall to the kitchen for another one, but was detoured by a blast behind him. The air in the hallway shivered.

Grey flung himself through the living room doorway as Simon shot the lock again. Grey heard the door slam open as he took the stairs at a dead run. Simon was through the front door now, bellowing. Grey's foot slipped and he went to all fours to gain the top of the stairs.

His intention, if he had one, was to get to the terrace and jump to the ground. But when he ran through the game room and threw himself against the terrace doors, they were locked. Grey screamed. The deadbolt lock demanded a key. Grey dug it out of his pocket and almost dropped it. His hand was shaking. He got the key into the lock but it wouldn't turn. The key wasn't a perfect fit with the new lock and he didn't have time to coax it. Grey no longer had any conscious thoughts. Simon was almost in the room with him. Grey kicked the door ineffectually and instinct threw him down behind the nearest shelter, though he knew it wouldn't save him. He crouched behind the pool table, hearing the screaming in the upstairs hall. Grey's hands were fumbling at the rack at this end of the table. It was full of billiard balls, hard and smooth as intentional weapons. He filled his hands.

The rage was on him again, the willingness to kill and die. When he heard Simon step through the door of the room he stood upright, simultaneously hurling the first ball. He didn't see whether it hit, didn't hear the rifle shots. He was launching ball after ball, whimpering with fear and anger. He knew he was dead but didn't feel the pain, throwing all the balls in his hands with incredible rapidity, wanting them all in the air at once before he lost his strength.

When his hands were empty he fell to the floor behind the pool table, panting and crying. Moans and cries filled the room. It would never be silent again. He would haunt this room, never slipping away, never be gone again. . . .

He *wasn't* gone, he noticed. His strength was ebbing, but he was alive. The idea wasn't pleasant. He wanted death, he had stood to embrace it, preferring unconsciousness to the fear and the expected pain. It wasn't fair to make him wait.

A minute might have passed before he sat up. He moved very slowly, not wanting to start his blood gushing. His hands moved very reluctantly over his body.

He was unhurt. With that knowledge, fear returned. He rose shakily and found himself alone in the room. No. He stepped around the table and saw Simon on the floor. Grey flinched back, then leaped toward him and wrenched the rifle out of his hands. There was no resistance. Grey stopped, put out a hand toward the staring face, then shrank from touching it.

Simon was perfectly still. His features looked slightly wrong, disarranged. One eye was sunk into his head and his nose was at a terrible, squashed angle. He would have been screaming in pain if he had still been alive.

Grey's throat clenched and he turned quickly away. The rifle clattered to the floor as he lunged toward the French doors. He felt his stomach swell again but he held it back as he jiggled the key until it turned and he threw open the doors. The fresh air revived him a little. He managed not to throw up. He sagged against the doorway and breathed deeply. The air didn't seem to find its way anywhere beyond his lungs. His knees remained weak, his hands shook.

Eventually he felt stronger and turned back into the room. He tried to leave his eyes glazed and his mind too dull to take in the scene, but he hesitated at the corpse, looking down into Simon's one good eye. Grey's body stirred again, and he didn't know whether he was going to cry, laugh, or throw up.

Then he heard footsteps coming up the stairs.

# 16

GREY'S FIRST THOUGHT WAS THAT IT MUST BE Judith coming home, and he moved to block her view of the corpse. But the footsteps on the stairs were unfamiliar. There were two sets, the first heavy, time-filling, coming down on every stair, the second a sharper, quicker echo. The sheriff was back, Grey thought. He must have stayed in the area and the shots had drawn him in. That was no part of Grey's plan. His heart jumped in panic. All thoughts of legal defenses were lost in a rush of guilty fear. He was alone in the room with a dead man, and he felt like a murderer. It was too soon to think of law. Grey stood dully, no plan forming. He found Simon's one staring eye and fixed on it. The two of them seemed to be tied together in a conspiracy to conceal their disagreement. But they were equally helpless. Waylon and Marcie walked into the room.

Marcie gasped so sharply at the sight of Grey it seemed he had frightened her. Grey stepped back. Marcie was startled anew when she looked down and saw Simon.

"My God," she said wonderingly. She knelt and touched the body. Grey took another step back. He was surprised to see Marcie with Waylon, and tried to think what it must mean.

Waylon had made no sound. His hands were empty. His eyes were fixed on his brother's corpse. He seemed unaware of the commanding position he held by filling the doorway.

When Marcie raised her eyes to Grey they were bright but not tearful. Her voice came from deeper in her throat than usual.

"We were driving by and we heard the noise. I thought you might need help. Waylon didn't want to stop, but I made him. I had no idea—"

Grey didn't respond. His eyes flickered to Waylon, who stood unmoving, then back to Marcie. She showed no inclination to move, and she seemed to have forgotten Simon already. She half-knelt casually on the floor within a foot of the body, frankly studying Grey's reactions. Her expression was more peaceful than the corpse's. She had found her spot.

"Let's go," Waylon said hoarsely. It was the first time he had spoken, and it sounded loud in the small room. Grey wanted to encourage their departure, but didn't say anything. Marcie was still watching him.

"In a minute," she said to Waylon. She stood up smoothly, but didn't move toward the door. The silence lengthened. Grey kept his face perfectly blank. Slowly, Marcie smiled. "What are you thinking?" she asked.

Grey shook his head. Waylon plucked at Marcie's sleeve. She kept smiling at Grey, but her voice was directed at Waylon: "He's thinking something."

Waylon stood watchfully behind her, still anxious to leave. Grey didn't look at him. It was true he was thinking, and he was afraid his thoughts would show on his face. He was thinking about the money, the loot from the robbery, almost forgotten in the rush of the last few days. Simon's persistence proved there had been money, and someone had taken it. Someone who might have wanted events to turn out just this way.

"What are you thinking?" Marcie asked again. Her tone was still light. Grey shook his head again. "Sure you are," she said. "You're a smart man. You have an idea, don't you? You'd like us to hurry out of here, wouldn't you?"

"I've got to call the sheriff," Grey said.

"Uh-huh. And tell him what?" she answered. "Tell him Simon sure did seem to believe that you had his money? But you didn't have it so somebody else must have? Something like that?"

"Shit!" Waylon said, coming out of his trance.

He grabbed Marcie's shoulders. "Why don't you shut up? First you had to come in and look, then you had to keep talking till—"

"It's okay," Marcie said. She shook off his hands. She was still smiling slightly, looking back at Grey, as she added to Waylon, "It just means they killed each other."

Grey was struck by her meaning before Waylon showed any reaction, but Waylon and Marcie were still blocking the doorway. Grey took a step back toward the French doors.

"It's better," Marcie said to Waylon. She was touching his arm, casually possessive. "We have to be careful." When he didn't move her tone sharpened. "He just killed your brother. Doesn't that mean anything to you?"

Now it was Waylon watching Grey. Waylon reached behind his back and brought a hunting knife into view. Marcie smiled as at a pupil with the right answer. She turned back toward Grey and shrugged slightly, her eyes ruefully apologizing. It wasn't a serious expression.

Waylon put his hands on Marcie's shoulders as if to move her aside. Grey glanced quickly at the pool table next to him. The balls were gone and the cue sticks were at the far end of the room. There was no weapon at hand. When he looked back he saw Waylon's hand moving, but then it stopped and the scene seemed unchanged. The difference was in Marcie's face. She looked slightly puzzled, trying to remember some small detail. She moved a hand slowly upward. And then the thin red line across her throat blossomed. The skin parted and blood welled out.

Her expression didn't turn fearful until her hand touched the blood and came away wet. Waylon released her shoulders and stepped away from her. She turned to look at him and shake her head. Her mouth opened, but she made no sound. She turned back to Grey, who stood frozen. One hand was clamped to her throat. Blood gushed between the fingers. Her grip tightened and her expression shifted as she turned away from Grey and put out a hand toward Waylon. She tried to snarl, and her hand clawed toward his face. Waylon backed away, frightened by the horror he had made of her. Marcie lunged toward and past him, making for the stairs, both hands holding her throat. Waylon shot one fast look at Grey and went after her.

Half a minute hadn't passed when Waylon returned to the room. He knew Grey hadn't come out, and there was no place to hide in the small room. But the French doors were now open. Holding the blade ahead of him at waist level, Waylon stepped through.

There was no one on the terrace, either. Waylon straightened and frowned. There were only a couple of flimsy chairs, nothing to hide behind, in the area enclosed by the wall. Beyond it the uninhabited hills were his only witnesses. Waylon walked to the wall at the right and looked over it. He saw Marcie's car parked in front of the house, and nothing else. He walked slowly back to the French doors and took one step inside.

Grey crouched outside the terrace wall, standing precariously on the metal connector block where the power line entered the house. A pool cue was in one hand, the fingers of the other hand gripping the top of the wall. He heard Waylon's disappearing footsteps and cautiously stood to look, shifting his weight slightly. There was a pop, a sudden sag, and the power line pulled loose. In an instant Grey was flailing toward the ground with a live wire falling with him.

Only luck let him avoid it until they hit the ground. Luckily again, Grey fell straight down, but the electrical wire fell toward its telephone pole at the back of the yard. Grey landed on his feet and fell immediately to the ground, not noticing the pain in his preoccupation with the power line. He poked at it with the pool cue and it danced away from him, toward its pole.

Of course he had screamed as he fell. When he was free of the wire he remembered his original problem and looked up. The house was dark, but a curious head was outlined against the stars. Grey scrambled to his feet and tried to run. Waylon threw a leg over the wall. But he stopped when Grey fell again, crying out and reaching for his right ankle, the one that had taken the force of his fall. Waylon watched as Grey struggled to rise and failed again. Waylon chuckled then, a small sound that drifted to Grey's ears, and the face disappeared from the terrace wall.

Waylon raced down through the dark house, ignoring the two bodies he passed. The brighter kitchen served as a beacon. He was through it and at the back door in moments. He was balked there by the deadbolt lock, and the small panes in the door would do him no good to break. He hesitated only a moment before grabbing up a kitchen chair and heaving it through the big window over the sink. He was right behind the chair, clambering up and leaping through the shattered window into the backyard.

Grey was no longer beside the house, but he couldn't have gone far. The moon and stars provided all the light one could want. Waylon saw Grey on the other side of the swimming pool, struggling to stand with the pool cue, of which he had made a clumsy crutch. Waylon breathed again and walked slowly toward the pool, careful not to let anything stop him.

Grey stood on the other side waiting for him. He had improved his position as well as he could, putting the largest obstacle in the yard between himself and his would-be killer. He couldn't run, but he could hobble a little with the pool cue, and as a last resort he could use it as a weapon. He was wondering if anyone would notice the torn power line, or if the sheriff would return. How long had it been since anyone had driven by the house? How long was it usually?

Waylon began circling the pool, and Grey moved in the opposite direction. Waylon paused.

"We've made a lot of noise," Grey called to him. "Somebody must be coming."

Waylon moved the other way. Grey compensated. He was sweating, and every step on his bad ankle seemed like the last one he could force himself to take.

"You can still get away," he shouted. "It'll look like Simon killed her and I killed him."

Grey had stopped, but Waylon was still moving. Suddenly he was running, around the end of the pool and onto Grey's side before Grey could take two more steps. It was hopeless. Grey flung the pool cue toward him and leaped into the water. At least he could move there, use his arms for locomotion. But he had nowhere to go. He flailed at the water desperately, straining for the opposite side.

Waylon skidded to a halt, started to run back the other way, then leaped into the water after his prey. The jump carried him to the middle of the pool. In that one movement he was almost on top of Grey. Waylon wasn't a good swimmer, but he pushed water away strongly, reaching toward the figure ahead of him.

Grey made the edge and pulled himself out. His right leg crumpled under him when he tried to stand, and he fell forward onto his face. Waylon was two strokes from the edge of the pool, the knife in his hand. Grey was too exhausted to rise again. He only had strength to grab the insulation of the power line that lay in front of him, turn over, and whip the broken end toward the pool.

Waylon screamed and leaped back. He realized his mistake and pushed forward again, almost touching the edge of the pool. The sizzling end of the power line dropped into the water directly in front of him.

Grey lay on his side, his expression betraying very little interest. Waylon arched straight upward, his scream backed by the crackle of the wire hitting the water. Sparks were the only lighting beneath the starry sky. At the top of his leap Waylon's scream stopped. Still stiff, he slid cleanly back into the water, bobbed once, and rolled over.

There was no more noise. The power line had shorted out, leaving only the stars and the moon lighting the yard. Grey lay still. There was no goal worth crawling toward. The darkness remained unbroken for a long time.

# EPILOGUE

PEOPLE CAME AS TO A WAKE. OLD FRIENDS KEPT alighting on the Stantons' front porch, wearing the expressions one would bring to comfort a widow, and sometimes carrying food or drink. A version of the story had appeared in the newspaper, which made Grey and Judith seem even more vulnerable, the house almost a tourist attraction. Visitors would glance surreptitiously around the living room looking for signs of damage, then turn the same glances on Judith and Grey and Katy. Everyone agreed they were putting on a brave, casual front.

Judith and Grey's favorite visitors were Harry and Fran, who exercised no subterfuge. "Don't it give you the creeps to be here at night?" Fran asked, her eyes searching their faces.

At least part of every visit was spent in

speculation, though eventually one of them would always say that they'd never know the whole truth.

"The part I keep wondering about," Fran said, "is why the brother killed that girl." She leaned forward on her chair.

Harry said to her, "You're looking at Grey like you expect him to confess he was the one who really killed her."

They all laughed and Fran slapped Harry's leg before she leaned back again, trying to look indifferent.

Grey had a new theory this week. "I think he was afraid of her," he said. "When they were here she seemed very much in charge. I wouldn't be surprised if she'd been behind it all—talked Waylon into taking the money, then sicced Simon off on me. I imagine she expected him to get sent back to prison instead of getting killed, but it worked out just as well. She adjusted to his death awfully fast. It was much more of a shock to Waylon to walk in and see him dead."

Fran was mulling it over, but didn't look convinced. "What do you think?" she asked Harry.

"I don't know why people kill each other," Harry said flatly. Fran looked at him curiously.

After a short silence Judith said, "I saw Lucinda Carmack at the store. She said she'd known Marcie years ago; Marcie used to be a customer of hers. From the way she said it I don't think she was talking about groceries."

"So Marcie probably knew Lucinda had that money at her store all along," Fran said.

"And must've already known Simon," Grey said, fitting this piece into his theory. "See? I wouldn't be surprised if she had put Simon up to that robbery in the first place. And then maybe was grooming Waylon to take Simon's place as soon as they got rid of him again."

Grey looked pleased with himself. He was leaning back on the sofa with his arm stretched out toward Judith. Katy was falling asleep between them. Her eyes were open, slowly revolving toward whichever adult was speaking, but the eyes' circuits were getting slower and slower. She made a faint noise to indicate she was still with them, and Grey put a hand on her head. Judith decided this would be a good time to tell him the other information she'd gotten from Lucinda.

"Lucinda told me something else." The others looked at her with polite interest. "She told me how much money it was that Simon stole from her in the first place." She paused, but didn't want to make the announcement too dramatic. "Twelve hundred dollars."

Harry shook his head. "Typical," he said. "People going to prison and getting killed over an amount of money that wouldn't keep 'em for a month."

"Hey, twelve hundred dollars is a lot of money to some people," Fran said.

"It would've been to Simon and Waylon," Judith agreed.

"But still, my goodness—" Fran began and trailed off.

Judith was watching Grey's bemused expression. It surprised him to learn what his life had been worth—and Simon's life, and Marcie's, and Waylon's. He thought about the three bundles of cash, five hundred dollars each, he had offered Simon to go away. Simon must have thought Grey would be willing to kill him rather than give up that much money. He shook his head and, seeing that his friends were watching him, told them what he was thinking. "I overpaid Simon."

"I think he would agree," Harry said.

Dusk had crept in while they talked. No cars passed, there was no one to be seen, and night shortened their view of the scene outside. They sat without turning on a light.

"I think someone's ready for bed," Judith said. She picked up the baby, murmuring reassurance to her, and climbed into the darkness up the stairs. Fran's eyes followed her.

"How can you stay in this house?" she whispered to Grey. "Doesn't she jump out of her skin every time a board creaks?"

"Where would we move to be safe? Back into the city? Every place we might move could have its own problems. Here we've already taken care of the problems. Besides, we like this house."

Fran studied his quiet smile, thinking that Grey had changed.

The sound of Judith's heels came down the stairs. Fran tried to make conversation with her. "What are you going to do now, honey?"

"Go back to work." Judith laughed. "You know how bored you can get spending all your time at home alone."

They had both turned weird, Fran decided. She and Harry declined dinner and departed rather soon after the invitation was made. Grey and Judith followed them outside, standing with their arms around each other's waists and waving. Fran waved back tentatively, then began talking to Harry as soon as the car doors closed.

Grey and Judith went back inside; Grey closed the front door behind them and followed Judith into the still-dim living room. In that light it was easy to remember the shambles the room had been very recently. Grey stopped with his hand on the light switch. The darkness appealed to him. The quiet confidence with which he had answered Fran's question seemed to him more than bravado. Grey felt changed. He still remembered, from that fearful night, those few moments when he had been suffused with a rage that made him eager to kill. Having experienced that emotion, he could not forget it, and couldn't escape a primitive pride in having defended his home. There was nothing in the shadows to be afraid of; *he* was the thing to be feared. In the darkness a low growl rose to his throat.

The effect was spoiled somewhat when his wife couldn't stop laughing for a full minute.